Broken Ponies
Sporting Pride #7
Charity Parkerson

Punk & Sissy Publications

Copyright

—Warning: This book is intended for readers over the age of 18. Some of my books contain allusions to past abuse and trauma.

Contents

Content

CONTENT WARNING: BROKEN PONIES deals with heavy topics such as sexual assault and mental health.

Introduction

THERE WAS A TIME when Buck planned to marry Sterling. Sterling shattered everything. He doesn't have any chances left to give.

Sterling grew up on a ranch. Horses are his everything now. As a professional polo player, he has his dream career. But it's starting to feel like a nightmare, closing in on him. He thinks maybe it's time to go home. Unfortunately, home is where his heart is, and he can't take back the way he left things with Buck. It's a hard choice between facing Buck again or facing his upturned life by going back to work. Both options leave him equally doomed.

Buck has worked the ranch for over a decade. He watched Sterling turn into an amazing horseman. Buck also fell in love so hard, it knocked the good sense from him. He knew to the bottom of his soul he would spend his life with Sterling. That is, until Sterling wrecked everything good about them. Now Sterling is back, and the feelings are still there, especially the hatred. Buck is pretty sure loving Sterling again will kill him.

Broken Ponies is the seventh book in Charity Parkerson's Sporting Pride series. These are sports-related romances, following men who find love while navigating high-profile careers. These are best enjoyed when read in order.

Chapter One

TWO WEEKS EARLIER

The rustling sound from inside the last horse's stall was as familiar to Buck as breathing. Someone brushed down the horses. The repetitive noise of a brush scraping downward over and over again was oddly loud tonight. There shouldn't be anyone left in the stables this late. That was exactly why he knew it was Sterling, and—unfortunately—he was the person Buck was looking for.

Buck headed for the back and peered inside. Obviously, he had known Sterling was back in town for a visit. But Buck had promised himself he would steer clear of any place he might run into Sterling. Leave it to Quince to fall out of commission and leave Buck no other choice but to end up here. He knew Quince wasn't really to blame, but he had to choose someone to take the fall.

"Don't you live in Miami now?"

Sterling glanced up. A smile spread across his lips, as if happy to see Buck. He loathed the way that fucked with his head. And those eyes, goddamn. "I still have a house here too, thankfully. If it wasn't in Tip's name, Mom likely would've sold it the second she noticed I was gone."

"You're safe, then. She likely never noticed." As the words left his lips, Buck regretted them. He saw the slight flinch they caused. Buck's throat swelled. He didn't want to feel anything but the rage Sterling had left behind.

Sterling being Sterling, he didn't give Buck the satisfaction of seeing how deeply his words cut. Sterling's mother didn't love him. That was no secret, but Buck had no business using that particular weapon against him.

"How are you enjoying being the new foreman? The position fits you."

"It's only temporary. I came out here to tell you Quince is awake. Now you have an excuse to go see that guard you have your eye on." Buck bit his tongue to keep from growling. He didn't want to show an ounce of jealousy. Tip's usual foreman, Quince, had recently been shot trying to protect his man. He had been in a coma for a while, and his man's new bodyguard was a little too sexy for Buck's comfort. Sterling could have anyone he wanted. Buck couldn't compete. Not that he wanted to.

Sterling tossed the brush aside and focused on Buck. Damn. He was still just sexy as fuck and... beautiful. His chest hurt. "Jealous?"

Buck snorted at Sterling's taunt. He hated how much he actually was. "You're still the same spoiled kid who thinks everyone wants him." Why? Seriously, why couldn't he shut up?

Sterling's eyes swept down Buck's body. "Not everyone. That's never been true. I still have a dildo named Buck that I can't get enough of."

In a flash, Buck sprang. He couldn't have stopped his feet from moving if he tried. Sterling's teasing had always been his downfall. "One of these days, being a tease will get you hurt."

Sterling untucked the T-shirt Buck wore beneath his unbuttoned flannel. He held Buck's stare as his hands slipped beneath the material.

Buck's skin was ablaze with lust. His body knew who touched him. Buck's heart knew.

"Quince won't choose to come back. He has Jathan now. You deserve the foreman position." Typical Sterling. Changing the subject the moment he broke Buck.

Buck didn't soften. A muscle in his jaw ticked. He couldn't hide his anger. "Don't try to make me want things I'll never have. That's all you ever do." Buck had sworn he would never be in that position again. Fuck. Sterling was just so goddamn beautiful.

Sterling slowly drew Buck closer. Pain and hatred rose inside Buck. There was no way Sterling didn't see the roiling emotions with the way he held Buck's stare. When their lips inevitably met, fire struck. Their kiss was violent. Buck wanted to die. He wanted Sterling to hurt. Still, his mouth moved to Sterling's neck, incapable of stopping. He had to taste his skin. Buck had to smell him. Everything Buck possessed missed Sterling.

"You still smell the same."

Buck dropped his forehead to Sterling's shoulder. The confession slaughtered him. His hatred grew by the second. Why did Sterling torment him like this? He had genuinely believed Sterling loved him before he left town. Now all Buck had was his broken heart, keeping him company.

"Tell me you hate me. It's okay. Say you don't even think about me because I make you sick. Tell me all the things I deserve to hear. It's okay."

Maybe it was time to say those things. Maybe if he did, he could move on. "You're right. I hate you." He shoved away from Sterling and didn't look back. He made it all of six feet from the stall. Buck froze. It was as if an invisible rope kept him tethered to the other half of himself. His dick strained against his zipper. Everything felt the same as before, except none of this life with Sterling actually existed. This was just Sterling filling a gap in his day. Sterling didn't understand how much he decimated Buck.

With a low curse, Buck spun. His angry stride carried him back to Sterling. He snatched Sterling off his feet and tossed him over his shoulder. Damn, he was light. Sterling had always been skinny, but this was ridiculous. It was like he hadn't eaten since he had been gone. It still pissed Buck off that he cared. He stormed across the way to an empty stall. Buck kicked open the door.

"Fuck you for this." The growled words sounded evil even to his ears. Buck couldn't stop. All the love was still there. His resentment had nowhere else to go.

Buck threw Sterling down on a pile of hay inside the stall and slammed the door behind them. The rage inside Buck had him falling on Sterling like a starving fiend. That was exactly what he was—famished for the pleasure only Sterling brought. Everything happened on autopilot as Buck fought to get what he wanted—to get off and then walk away. He needed Sterling to suffer—left empty and betrayed. The way he had done Buck.

Buck didn't slow or even recall anything he had done until he slammed inside Sterling. His gaze moved down Sterling's body. Buck had him facedown and ass up with no mercy for Sterling's discomfort on the rough hay. He wished his actions made him feel better. They didn't. He was still broken. All the nights he had stroked himself and whispered Sterling's name crashed into him. Buck needed to make Sterling pay for every pang in Buck's soul. Buck shut down his mind and fucked Sterling hard. In the back of his mind, Buck realized he would regret not taking this final opportunity to savor every second. But all Buck could think was at least this wasn't another fury-filled night of masturbation. At least this was real.

Chapter Two

THE SMELL OF FRESH hay surrounded Sterling. He couldn't count the number of times he had hidden in the hayloft as a kid. Sterling didn't know why he'd thought he needed to hide. No one had been looking for him. When Sterling's dad had died, so too had their family. Sterling had ceased to exist. Living on a ranch hadn't given him the opportunity to stir up too much mischief, but he couldn't count the number of times he hoped, if he stayed hidden long enough, his mom might actually realize he was gone. He had slept many a night in the thick hay. It wasn't technically comfortable, but the rough bedding wasn't the worst either. When Sterling had gotten older, rolling in the hay had become a very different experience.

Sterling rolled onto his side and stared at nothing, getting stabbed in the ribs by straw and seeing only the images inside his head.

Everything about Buck was beautiful. His hard body. The way his blue eyes always stared at Sterling with hunger. But nothing about the giant cowboy stood out as much as the way he made Sterling feel. It wasn't always good. Today was one of those days that left him torn. He still floated on a cloud, relaxing in Buck's arms, basking in the afterglow of euphoria.

Buck toyed with Sterling's fingers. He traced a circle around Sterling's ring finger. "We should get married before you go."

Sterling went completely still inside. "You'd have to tell AJ about us. I know we decided to hide this together, but we can't pretend an entire marriage doesn't exist, most especially from your son."

"I know."

Sterling heard the sadness in Buck's voice. It was like getting punched in the chest. Buck genuinely sounded as if he had carried some small hope Sterling would agree to a whole-ass clandestine marriage. What the hell? Sometimes, Buck really knew how to hurt him in a way no one else did. That was saying a lot. Sterling's entire family acted like he hadn't been born. At first, with Buck, it hadn't seemed like a big deal to stay quiet. What was one more person treating him as if he was nothing going to matter? It did. More than with anyone else, it did. Sterling couldn't do this anymore.

Sterling rolled upward and eyed the loft. He had spent so many heated nights here, and even more heartbroken ones. He should just go home to Miami. Sterling didn't have much left for him there, but he didn't hurt like this there. At least, he hadn't for the past three years. That wasn't true any longer.

The sound of a loud diesel engine had Sterling moving to his feet. He pushed the doors open so the incoming hay could easily be lifted into the loft. He stared at the ground below for a second. It wasn't that far down. Sterling still wondered what would happen if he jumped. As a kid, he had been convinced if he leapt from the upper storage area, he would die—like plunging to his death from a high rise. He had considered it more nights than not. Sterling had been lonely. Still was, honestly. But he had also been a dramatic kid, willing to do anything for someone to see him. That willingness hadn't stopped at adulthood. Now he was darker inside than ever.

He stepped back, making room for the stacked bales. Sterling put on his work gloves and got started on unloading. He moved the first stack to the back corner. Unlike most people, he didn't mind this part of farm work. It was a mindless task, ensuring they could get as much hay as possible stored off the ground and out of the weather.

"Damn. When are you going back to Miami?"

Even though Sterling's racing heart tried leaping into his throat, he somehow managed to hide his surprise. He hated people sneaking up on him. Sterling tossed a quick glance Buck's way as he headed for another bale. "Not sure."

Buck went to work beside him. "You were always one to jump in and help. I couldn't get AJ to do shit."

"Not everyone cares for ranch life. How is AJ, anyhow?" Sterling didn't look at Buck as he made the inquiry.

"Still living in the city. He has some sort of computer job, working for the government." Sterling glanced over in time to see Buck shrug. "He doesn't talk much about it, so that's all I really know. Of course, you know AJ, he doesn't talk much about anything. He always asks about you every time we talk."

Sterling nodded, acknowledging the words. "Be sure to tell him I said hi."

Silence fell between them. Sterling despised this part. He used to tease and flirt. Buck used to watch him with more hunger than Sterling knew how to handle back then. Now he knew exactly what it took to take on

Buck. Unfortunately, no one hated Sterling more... except for Sterling.

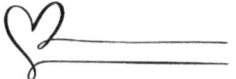

Buck fought for his life. He had been such a crazy mixture of emotions for years with Sterling. Sterling had moved to Miami three years ago, and Buck hadn't moved on. He no longer knew which of them was the most to blame. All Buck knew was he had fallen hard in love with Sterling seven years ago and obsession's grip hadn't released his throat since. The guy was only four years older than his son, for fuck's sake. He was twenty-six to Buck's forty-four. Buck had been aware of that every single moment since he realized Sterling's nonstop flirting was real. It had been Sterling's nineteenth birthday. Buck hadn't meant to fall so hard in love, especially since loving Sterling was the worst thing to ever happen to him.

"I can go back to Miami now, if you want."

The quietly spoken words yanked Buck from his dark thoughts. He felt like absolute shit. Two weeks ago, he had thrown Sterling into the hay and fucked him hard, punishing him for the past. He knew damn well his anger was a dark cloud that choked everything around him, including Sterling. Sometimes, he wasn't sure which of them was the bad guy. It was Buck. He was the older one. Buck was the one who was supposed to know better. Still, he never could bend and admit his faults. Sterling knew them, though.

"This is your home. I'm just an employee."

Silence met his words, forcing him to look Sterling's way. That turned out to be a mistake. Sterling didn't show his heart. But when he did, what he saw always punched him in the chest, because no matter what else Buck felt, he loved Sterling. The split second of soul-crushing unhappiness he saw wasn't swiftly hidden by a mask of indifference as quickly as he was sure Sterling intended.

Sterling looked away first. He took off his work gloves and shoved them in his back pocket. Sterling headed for the ladder without looking back. Buck's chest hurt. He tilted his chin to the ceiling and slowly blew out his breath. When it came to Sterling, he never knew what to do. For him, Sterling meant much-needed laughter and off-the-chart passion. Buck had hopped through his fair share of beds of various varieties over the years. Doing that shit was how he became a single father. Sterling was different than anyone else for Buck. Before Sterling, Buck hadn't realized exactly how hard he could fall in love. He also hadn't known how big of a selfish asshole that particular state of being would make him. Buck would have done anything to keep Sterling to himself, except that wasn't what he had done. Instead, he had kept Sterling like an embarrassing secret. Sterling had been right to leave.

"You won't even know I'm gone."

The ache in Buck's chest said otherwise. "That's not true at all."

Sterling swiped a sweet kiss across Buck's lips. "You know I'll come back as often as I can. I can't stay away from you."

"Maybe you should."

"Hey, Dad."

Buck jumped back so fast, he didn't know how he didn't fall. He turned, pasting on a bright smile for AJ. "Hey. What's up? You never step foot in the barn."

If AJ had seen anything, he didn't show it. AJ shrugged. "Dean's parents are flying to Hawaii for the weekend. They asked me to join them, and I didn't want to just disappear without a word."

AJ was nineteen. While he still lived at home while going to college, he didn't truly owe Buck any explanations. AJ was an adult now. However, Buck was grateful he still told him things, and didn't have him filing missing person's reports. It would suck to be stuck worrying. "That sounds nice. Have fun for me too. I've always wanted to go there." Which AJ knew since his best friend's ridiculously rich parents had taken AJ countless times over the years.

AJ's gaze slid Sterling's way before moving back to hold his stare. It wasn't a knowing look—more like he weighed his words since they weren't alone. "Well, we'll have to figure out how to go sometime. But this trip means I'll be out of the house for a few days. You'll actually have the place to yourself. Maybe you should bring home some trouble or something."

Sterling chuckled, but the sound of his laughter moved away from them.

Buck panicked a little over Sterling slipping away from him before he finished their conversation.

"Who knows? Maybe I will. Surely, I'm not too old for someone in this town to want me."

A bright smile lit AJ's face. He looked just like his mom. "That's the spirit." He took a step back. "See you in a few days. Love you."

Buck smiled. "Have fun. I love you too." He barely made it long enough for AJ to leave before he spun. His heart slowed from its terrified state when he saw Sterling had moved to his horse's stall, babying his baby. He hadn't left yet.

Buck moved to the stall door. "Well, you heard the boy. You have to stay now. We have two whole nights alone."

Sterling didn't smile the way Buck hoped. "Two whole nights," Sterling quietly repeated without looking his way.

A pit opened in Buck's stomach. The closer they got to Sterling actually leaving him for pro polo, the more this chasm between them grew. Buck closed his eyes and prayed for strength. This was Sterling's dream coming true.

Unfortunately, Sterling found his words before Buck did. "You want me to give up *my entire career for two nights of your guilt-ridden sex."*

It hadn't been a question. Sterling had made up his mind about them.

Buck released an uncomfortable-sounding laugh. "Making love to you has never been guilt-ridden."

They equally knew that was a lie. Buck had begged Sterling a million times to marry him while also showering him with love, but they knew the truth. Sterling might be the one leaving, but Buck hadn't truly been there at all.

Sterling was twenty-six now. That didn't seem so bad. Unfortunately, before they ended, they had thoroughly wrecked each other. There was no taking that back.

Chapter Three

DIM LIGHTING AND NEON beer signs made the honky-tonk roadside bar and grill seem more intimate than it should. Sterling had never realized that until he sat across from German. Tip's foreman had fallen in love with a pretty damn famous basketball player. They had hired the security company German worked for and German was the guard working more often than not. Considering they lived in the middle of nowhere on Tip's ranch, German didn't have to do much. The first time Sterling met German, German had called him a boy. For whatever reason, they hit it off immediately. They were friends. Sterling desperately needed that now, even if he couldn't confess why.

"When do you head back to Miami?"

Sterling chewed his bottom lip for a second. He couldn't think of anything to say other than the truth. "I'm not sure if I'm going back."

German blinked, keeping his face expressionless. "Isn't this thing you do damn near impossible to achieve, considering how small the teams are? You're obviously one of the best of the best to be where you are. You have a year left on your contract. Why wouldn't you go back?"

Sterling searched his mind for a way to explain without giving away his secrets. "You're right about how hard it is. Unfortunately, it's also ruined my life."

German's light blue gaze sharpened. "How so?"

Sterling rubbed the back of his neck and looked around before meeting German's stare again. "Do you mind if we talk about something else?"

German went from having his elbows on the table, leaning Sterling's way, to sitting back to openly study him.

Sterling fought the urge to squirm. German had a very penetrating stare. Sterling couldn't take it. "Tell me more about yourself. We always talk about me."

German snorted. "I do that for a reason. If we can't talk about your career, let's talk about Buck."

Sterling's throat swelled. His gaze bored into German. He tried to sound nonchalant. "What about Buck?" German shouldn't know about Buck. No one should.

"What's up with that guy? Did you accidentally kick his dog sometime, or what? I know you wouldn't do that on purpose, but damn. He gives you some looks."

That stung, and it seemed that was exactly what he needed. He wasn't projecting or imagining things. Buck hated him. "We were a couple before I moved. He was embarrassed to be dating me and kept me a secret. All while swearing we would get married someday." German didn't look surprised or judgmental, so Sterling kept talking. "Right before I left, he begged me to marry him before leaving, but somehow, he still thought he could keep a whole husband hidden. So, I walked away and stayed gone. His cowardice broke me. I went from being an already fucked-up guy to self-destructive. I very publicly dated every celebrity I could." Sterling held German's stare. He needed German to see exactly how serious he was. Sterling needed to say all the things, and the dam was gone now. "I wanted him to hurt the way I hurt and know exactly what it felt like to have someone make him feel like he didn't exist. It wasn't right, but I'm not sure I'm a very good person, so." Sterling shrugged.

To his surprise, German didn't look like he thought any less of Sterling. "Why was he embarrassed to be with you? You're amazing."

A sad smile tugged at the corners of his mouth. Sterling couldn't hold on to it. "I'm nearly the same age as his son. We even went to the same school together at one point and everything."

"So?"

A genuine smile snapped to Sterling's lips. "Yeah. That's what I thought too. It seems I was wrong. My age mattered to him, and he broke something in me I couldn't afford to lose."

German cocked his head to one side, looking a little too scrutinizing for Sterling's comfort. "Why do you sound like you're still heartbroken over something that happened three years ago?"

Pain welled in his chest. "Three years is nothing when the love is real."

"So you still want him?"

Sterling desperately wanted to be done with this. "Yes. I guess a part of me always will. Unfortunately, I'm still the secret shame and I'm not sure we don't hate each other now. We can't be fixed."

German's chest expanded on a deep breath. "Well, on that note. We should get something stronger than beer. Quince said we should have fun, and he's more than willing to pick us up if we get shitfaced. I say we take him up on the offer. It sounds like you need to forget for a little while."

Sterling couldn't stop smiling. It felt good to get everything off his chest. He didn't have anyone he could talk to about Buck. Maybe that was all he had needed to move on. He felt lighter.

"Absolutely."

German waved down a server and ordered shots. Sterling stared at him in a new light. They really were friends. He wasn't alone.

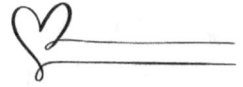

Despite the noise surrounding him, the thin wood panel behind his head did nothing to mute Sterling's every damning word in the booth behind him. They sat back-to-back and Buck hung on to every confession. Guilt gnawed at his gut. It was bad enough that he was basically stalking Sterling. He couldn't claim his choice of seating was a coincidence. When Sterling had left the property with German, Buck had to know. He had to see Sterling flirt with someone else, so maybe he could walk away. Unfortunately, now he couldn't breathe. He hadn't realized how much he had been hurting Sterling back in those days. Love had made him blind and dumb. He had never felt the way he felt about Sterling. Not before or after. Sterling was a sickness. An old fool's dream come true. Until Sterling popped back up in his life a few weeks ago, Buck had forgotten how much Sterling made him feel. Now Buck couldn't stop. He was back to acting crazy all over again. Buck needed a drink.

Three beers in, it hit him. Sterling had never been ashamed of them. All the times he saw the hurt in Sterling before he hid it again flitted through Buck's mind. His chest hurt and determination grew with each passing second. He was the problem. Buck had always been the true villain in their story. Sterling should hate him. Yet Sterling had told German he still loved Buck. Buck didn't deserve it, but fuck. He wanted that love with every fiber of his being. Buck had felt the loss and betrayal. He deserved to have a goddamn life outside of being a father. His son was grown. Sterling was too. They were all fucking adults. He deflated as quickly as his courage grew. Sterling was Tip's baby brother. Tip was Buck's boss. He didn't know what to do.

Buck's gaze slid toward the dance floor. Sterling had dragged German into a line dance and tried teaching him the steps.

They laughed uproariously every time German missed a step or turned the wrong direction. Damn. Sterling really was amazing. His whole life, people had fucked over Sterling. But Sterling kept coming back for more abuse, because attention was attention, and Sterling had never gotten that. He had the world's eyes on him now. No matter what he said, Buck wanted that for Sterling. Sterling deserved it. He made Buck proud as hell.

Buck chuckled when a busty server in a ripped, tight t-shirt appeared with more shots. Sterling and German smiled as they accepted. They tossed back the shots. The woman took one with them. A slow song started. Their new friend set her serving tray aside and motioned for German to dance with her. Sterling's smile never dimmed as he watched German accept.

Buck couldn't say what happened. He was on his feet and moving in Sterling's direction without a single thought. The moment Sterling spotted him, the air shifted. Sterling went from smiling to smoldering in under a second. Buck didn't know what Sterling saw in Buck's expression, but he didn't move. This wasn't a gay bar. Men didn't dance with other men here. Buck didn't consider that or anything else. He had Sterling in his arms with zero cares for the rest of the world. Sterling held on to him like a life preserver—like he was a drowning man. Too late, Buck realized that was exactly what he was to Sterling. Every epiphany made him feel and look worse and worse. He had murdered something as close to perfect as love got. But that emotion still choked the life from him.

Buck's lips skimmed the shell of Sterling's ear. He heard Sterling's breathing change.

Sterling's fingertips dug deeper into Buck's skin. Buck's throat swelled. He didn't know how to fix them. All he knew was how he felt.

"I'm sorry for everything. You deserve better than me."

A ragged-sounding breath escaped Sterling.

Buck couldn't stop. "There's no reason for you to believe. I've never given you any reason to feel secure and loved with me. But goddamn, Sterling. I love you so much. It makes me insane and jealous and angry all the way back around to just drowning in how much I love you. My feelings for you make me feel like some sort of psychopath. I don't know what I'm saying or asking right now. I just really need this dance."

"Okay."

The response sounded so small and weak. Buck's eyes burned. He practically felt the way Sterling couldn't trust him not to destroy him, but he gave Buck what he needed, anyway. How had Sterling lived like this? The inside of his head must be a painful mess. People just crushed him over and over, and Sterling begged for more. That included Buck. Buck no longer knew who he was the angriest with. The entire world had failed Sterling. Buck couldn't keep adding his name to the list.

His throat burned, but Buck needed to say more. No matter how much it hurt, Sterling deserved more. "You look genuinely happy with German. Maybe you should hang on to that. You deserve to have the whole world at your feet."

Sterling didn't respond.

Buck's lips lightly skimmed Sterling's.

The song ended and Buck headed for the door without looking back or making eye contact with anyone. Maybe that was the goodbye he should have given Sterling three years ago. Maybe they would be free from this by now if he had. He supposed they would never know. But better late than never to do the right thing. Buck needed to get back to living his life shut down and on autopilot. Sterling needed to get back to being young. At least one of them needed peace. It should be Sterling.

Chapter Four

HE SMELLED THE SAME. That was always the thought that owned Sterling the most every time he touched Buck. His sexy scent lived in Sterling's heart and brought out every ounce of nostalgia when he smelled it. Every day, Sterling just sank deeper into confused despair. He didn't understand anything anymore. All he had ever known was he loved Buck with every breath he took. Sterling didn't know how to let it go even as he recognized their toxic love was killing him.

He paced his house. Why had he thought coming home would soothe him? Mostly, he had thought he would feel safe here, if not welcomed. Sterling didn't feel safe anymore anywhere. Every noise made him jump. He couldn't sleep. Images rolled through his mind that made his stomach churn. Being here wasn't helping anything. All he saw were the days his family pretended he didn't exist. Tip had built him this house on the ranch to give him a place to escape their mom. But then he had gone right back to his life as this huge soccer player, traveling all over the place. Sterling had lost himself in his horses and Buck back then. Now neither of those things belonged to him anymore. Truth be told, they hadn't been his back then either.

Sterling stopped in the center of his living room. The moonlight coming through the windows cast enough light to illuminate the room. Everything looked cold and unwelcoming. Nothing and nowhere felt like home. Anger, bitterness, hatred, and fury pulsed inside him, getting bigger by the second. The way Buck had whispered his love and walked away again kept playing through his mind. He didn't know what was wrong with him. Sterling didn't understand why everyone got their kicks from his pain. He didn't want this life. Sterling hadn't asked for it. His existence was a huge joke, and the laugh was at his expense.

Without thinking or gathering a plan, Sterling yanked open the coat closet and grabbed a bat from his ball bag. This time, he paced the house, searching. He had to cut this thing from his soul that made him so fucking easy to walk on. He didn't want to be weak. Sterling didn't want to live at all anymore. That revelation sent the helpless rage overboard. Sterling swung, destroying every trophy he had ever won. His eyes darted in every direction. What else? He needed to crush anything and everything that had allowed him to lie to himself. To pretend he could be special. He was too far gone to think clearly. Sterling was stuck on self-destruct. He smashed everything, breaking everything until it looked the way he felt. He caught a quick glimpse of himself in the mirror. Fuck that. He hated that guy. Glass flew in his face and cut through his skin as his bat smashed into the mirror over and over again, doing nothing to squelch the rage and pain.

Sterling had no idea how long his tirade lasted. In the end, he was left standing in the center of a home that finally matched him on the inside. Tears mixed with blood to trail down his face. He deflated. Sterling was left with nothing but the truth. He was done. Sterling had officially tried every lifeline to save himself, but the answer was clear now. He shouldn't have been born. His existence was unnatural. Sterling was too weary to go on. He touched his lips. Buck had kissed him goodbye. It was time to go.

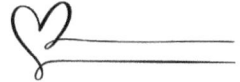

Buck kept one eye out, hoping to spot a flash of strawberry-blond hair. He ached to look into Sterling's light green eyes again. Maybe Buck would never get to touch Sterling again, but the thought of not getting to see him was a weight sitting on his chest. A movement at the edge of his vision had Buck's head whipping toward the barn door. Tip strolled inside with his forehead furrowed. Buck couldn't decide if the guy was angry or worried. Either way, Buck had a bad feeling he should make himself scarce. Tip was Sterling's big brother. Maybe Sterling had finally taken their issues to him. That was his right. Unfortunately, this was Buck's job and home.

Buck almost took a step back when Tip's long stride brought him Buck's way. "Have you seen Sterling?"

Oh, no. Buck swiped his sweaty palms on his thighs. "No. Why?"

Tip shook his head. "He was supposed to meet me for breakfast over an hour ago. I've tried calling and texting, but he's ignoring me."

Fuck. Without a single thought or care for how he looked, Buck darted from the barn.

Tip was right on his heels. "What the fuck, Buck?"

Buck motioned toward the closest farm truck. "Get in."

His mind raced as Tip barely made it inside the vehicle before Buck was off.

"Seriously, Buck. What's wrong?"

Buck tried to explain through the panic that choked him. "He hasn't been right since he came home. I thought it was maybe just me. Last night, I overheard him saying he might not return to Miami. He refused to give a reason. But there was something in his voice." Buck shook his head. "I don't know. He's just... not who he used to be," Buck finished lamely. He was too panicked to think clearly enough to explain.

"He doesn't plan to return to—"

Tip's words died an abrupt death and Buck's heart dropped to his shoes when Sterling's front door came into view. The screen door stood wide open, blowing slightly back and forth with the wind. The front door stood just as wide.

Buck barely had the truck in park before he leaped from the vehicle. He hit the ground running at full speed. His feet froze so abruptly when he reached the door, he almost fell on his face. The place looked like a tornado had ripped through. A baseball bat sat in the center of the destruction. It might not have stood out if it wasn't covered in blood.

"Holy shit."

Since Buck's throat was nearly swollen shut, he let Tip's outburst speak for him as well.

Tip rushed through the house and darted from room to room before returning to the living room. "He's not here, but every single room is trashed. There's more blood in the bedroom."

They met and held each other's stare. Buck knew they were on the same page. Sterling had finally let the demons win.

Tip broke first. He whipped out his phone. "Call everyone. Let's spread out and search the property."

Buck nodded along. "You call the police. I'll try his phone and pray he'll answer me."

They gave each other a sharp nod.

Tip stepped outside while Buck dug out his phone. He paced while he pulled up Sterling's number. "Please don't be dead. Please fucking answer." Buck repeated the chant as he hit the call icon.

A ringing sounded in the distance. Buck followed the sound to Sterling's bedroom. There was a hell of a lot more blood than Tip had let on. In the middle of Sterling's obliterated trophies, Sterling's phone rang and vibrated across the floor. Buck went down on his haunches and scooped it from the mess. The screen was heavily shattered, and Buck's name flashed through the cracks. Actually, it said, *My Love*. Buck disconnected the call. Sterling's phone stopped ringing. He sniffed. The shock slowly melted, and reality struck. Sterling had really done it. He had gone to the only place Buck couldn't follow. Maybe Buck wouldn't last much longer either.

Chapter Five

QUIET PRESSED SO HARD on Buck's eardrums, he thought he might go deaf. He continued sweeping Sterling's house long past clearing up the mess. Buck didn't want Sterling to find a single sliver with his bare feet when he came home. He had to believe Sterling would be back. The alternative was unthinkable.

Buck had offered to stay behind and clean. Also, in case Sterling came home while everyone else searched the property. If they found Sterling dead, Buck couldn't be there for that. He had already run through every scenario in his head. Now he was just exhausted. Buck's chest hurt like never before. This was his fault. Buck had to own that. Sterling had always been a ray of sunshine, acting goofy and making everyone laugh. He was irresistible. Buck didn't think he could be blamed for falling in love. Everything that happened afterward, that was him. He had broken Sterling down and demolished everything good inside of him. The worst part was Buck was the adult. Buck had raised a son to adulthood. He knew better. In his eyes, Sterling had always been grown. Despite him bringing everyone else happiness, when no one watched, he turned serious, and his eyes changed. Buck had seen the unhappiness and never stopped to think maybe he was the one causing it. The least he could do was clean. He had nothing else to offer.

The front door opened.

Buck nearly hit his knees in relief until he realized it was Tip. Something died inside him at Tip's expression. He looked tired, stressed, and heartbroken. Buck couldn't move. He couldn't speak. Everything inside him was poised on the edge of a knife.

Tip moved to the couch and sat. He met Buck's stare. Buck swore the man saw him all the way to his soul. "The police found him."

That one line had Buck ready to step into traffic.

Thankfully, Tip kept talking without making Buck ask. "He was walking aimlessly down Old Country Road. They say he was nude and covered in blood. They said he was practically nonverbal. Once they determined the blood was his, they called for an ambulance."

Buck had a million questions, but he was too scared to ask. If he opened his mouth, everything inside him might fall out.

Tip's chest expanded as he took a deep breath. His stare seemed to deepen. "It's time for everyone to stop pretending you're not involved with my brother."

The statement finally shook Buck from his shock. He opened his mouth. Buck had no idea what he planned to say. Everything inside him screamed for him to deny it. His tongue refused to tell that lie.

Tip held up his hand, stopping him. "This isn't your fault."

Buck snapped his mouth closed. He couldn't even think clearly anymore.

Tip kept going. "He's having a manic episode."

Buck sat.

Tip eyed him. "By your reaction, I assume you didn't know Sterling is bipolar."

Buck shook his head. His voice still wouldn't work.

Tip nodded, as if he expected as much. "Unfortunately, there's more. Under most circumstances, I'd never tell you all this, but I honestly think you love him." He took no mercy on Buck. "It seems he purposely stopped his medication about a month after coming home. He wanted the intrusive thoughts to finally drive him over the edge."

"Why?" It was all Buck could croak out. There was so much pain in that one word that even Buck flinched. He didn't know why he asked why. Buck knew. It was him.

Tip took a shaky-sounding breath and rubbed the center of his chest, as if absently trying to scrub away the pain. "It seems, after their final match of the season, the team's head coach drugged Sterling and sexually assaulted him."

Buck wanted to die. For so many reasons, he wanted death to take him. He swallowed. "I didn't know." Buck lasted half a second. "Did he call the police? Was this reported?"

Tip shook his head. "He didn't have any definitive proof. In fact, he blames himself. Sterling says you always told him his careless flirting would get him hurt." Tip held his stare like he recorded every minute detail of Buck's reaction. Buck watched the realization grow in Tip that maybe Buck was to blame after all. Tip didn't slow. He kept ripping Buck's heart out. "The thing is, it's not careless flirting. It's a nervous tick. Fear of people dismissing his existence. He doesn't know how to connect with people. No one gave him love when he needed it the most. He wasn't taught what healthy love looks like. His entire life, he's been rejected by everyone. The only attention he's ever gotten was from polo and being sexualized. I failed him."

Buck stared at nothing, seeing nothing except all the ways he had punished Sterling since he came home. That night in the hay. Goddamn. "If you want my resignation, you can have it."

Tip snorted. "I have no doubt Sterling pursued you with everything he has. The only time I heard any emotion in his voice tonight was anytime he said your name." Tip shook his head. He looked every bit as shell-shocked as Buck felt.

Buck couldn't take it anymore. "What now?"

Tip startled, as if he fell into his thoughts and forgot about Buck. His eyes looked haunted when he focused on Buck. He cleared his throat. "The hospital will keep him until his meds have him stabilized again.

After that, I don't know. He doesn't want to come back here, but, according to him, he can't go back to Miami. I just don't know." Tip stood. "But I know one goddamn thing, after I go home and hug my husband, I'm about to have my foot so far up a coach's ass, he'll be the one wishing for death."

Buck felt the same rage Tip did, but the pain and guilt eclipsed everything. He felt too fucking helpless to move.

Tip headed for the door.

Buck spoke without thinking. "I do love him, you know. You're right about that. I'll do whatever it takes to help."

Tip gave him a sharp nod and left Buck alone with the destruction he had caused. Buck would never forgive himself for this. Every dark thought led to another until he had to fight the urge to head to Sterling's mom's house and put her down like a dog. Her shitty parenting started everything.

Buck dug out his phone and called his son. He needed AJ to know he was loved and accepted in every way and always would be.

AJ answered on the third ring. "Hey, Dad. What's up?"

"I love you."

An uncomfortable-sounding chuckle tumbled through the line. "I love you too. What's wrong?"

Tears welled in his eyes. Buck had no one to lean on. He couldn't tell AJ the things Tip had told him. But he could do one thing he should've done years ago. "There's something I need to tell you."

It was easier than he expected. In the face of so much horror, loving someone nearly half his age seemed like nothing. Everything started with no one loving Sterling the way he deserved. Buck would be goddamned if Sterling ever felt that way again. It was time for that healthy love Tip mentioned.

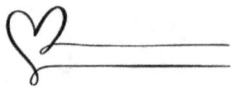

All he did was sleep. Sterling couldn't help it. It was like his months of silence, rage, pain, and depression had finally caught him and crushed him. He was alone. Sterling always was, though. Sometimes he preferred the silence. He hated feeling like he had to be funny or talkative out of fear of someone not wanting to be his friend anymore. Then, when they left, he second-guessed everything he said and did, certain he made an idiot of himself, and they would block his number. He felt like an inconvenience. Life wasn't easier alone, but at least he could sit in silence, only being judged by himself. That was why he had told the hospital to refuse visitors. He had nothing left to give.

Sterling supposed the meds were working again. Honestly, he couldn't tell any longer. He didn't enjoy anything anymore anyhow. Sterling simply took up space and racked up medical bills. Maybe he should move somewhere with universal healthcare. Maybe Canada. Nah. It was too cold. Sterling had gotten accustomed to the Florida heat. Now he wore a jacket when it hit sixty-five degrees. He would say Australia, but the spiders were huge. Maybe Spain. Did they even have universal healthcare? That wasn't a bad idea if they did. Sterling had to think about anything at all. He needed to look toward the future. Sterling had a bad feeling the whole world was about to know his business and see him as only a victim now. Polo didn't create many household names. He wasn't really famous or anything. It was possible this entire thing would barely be a blip on the news. No matter what, Sterling didn't want to be here anymore. Since it seemed he wasn't really brave enough to off himself, he would need a new plan. Sterling could work on that and busy his mind.

A perfunctory knock landed on the door before it opened. A nurse appeared with a shot and a gift bag. Sterling watched the woman move his way, feeling absolutely nothing. She had purple hair and tattoos. Those were always the best caretakers.

She handed him the bag. "This is for you."

Sterling checked the name on her badge as she passed the bag along. Shelby. "Thank you."

Shelby flashed him a smile. "No problem. Now, I'm going to flush your line first, but I have more meds. It seems the doctor has ordered for you to still get everything intravenously."

A humorless laugh burst out. "I'm not to be trusted to take pills."

She patted his shoulder. "Everyone forgets to take their meds occasionally."

Sterling allowed the falsehood to stand. He simply let the influx of drugs keep him mellow. Sterling had nowhere to go anyhow. When he was alone again, he stared at the bag on his lap. It was shiny blue and lightweight for its large size. He gave up trying to decide who might have sent it and moved the tissue paper aside. A smile exploded across his face. It was the Bakugan battle set he had begged Santa for when he was a kid. His dad had died that year. His mom had shut down. Tip had left to enjoy his new freedom and career. His sister cried all the time and Sterling had just sort of disappeared. He hadn't wanted to bother anyone with a Christmas list. No one listened when he spoke anyhow. Sterling hadn't been worried, though. He had told Santa. There hadn't been a single doubt he would get the only gift he wanted. Then Christmas had come, and he watched Miranda open a million presents while he waited patiently for his one lonely package under the tree. Turned out it was from a great aunt he had never met. It was a sweater. She had knitted it herself, which was fine, but it was about three sizes too small. The way he felt that day had stuck with him. Even though he had been twelve and had fully known Santa Claus wasn't real, there had still been some small hope inside him that life wouldn't fail him just the one time. There was only one person who knew that story. A letter was taped to the box. Sterling stared at the folded paper for much longer than necessary. His hand shook when he finally peeled the note off and unfolded it.

Sterling,

I actually bought this for you three Christmases ago. Well, you know why you didn't get it then. I found it in the closet. It was past time I should've given it to you. When you left, I was so angry with myself for not telling everyone about us, so maybe you'd finally take mercy on me and marry me. I was scared as hell people would think I was some pervert, since my son isn't that much younger than you. Plus, I was terrified Tip would fire me and I'd have no way to support you. Mostly, I just knew you could do better than me. I knew, if we got married, you'd get to Miami and have men way better and younger than me throwing themselves at your feet. You'd stay faithful because that's who you are, and I would've cursed you to some sort of half life. Not once have I ever known what the right thing to do is. All I've ever known is that I love you. For real. All the way to my soul. That means putting you first. Except, maybe my idea of putting you first was the wrong one. I don't know. All I know is I fucked up so goddamn royally and I've been nothing but miserable since you left. You love your career. You earned that and deserve everything you've accomplished. I just wish so damn badly I had found the courage not to be left behind because I'll never stop loving you. That love is something I wake up with every day and take to bed every night. I don't even know the point of this letter. Just please don't leave me. Just please be happy. If you need a Bakugan partner, just let me know. I'm pretty sure all AJ's old battle brawlers are still around here somewhere. Somehow, I still step on one about every six months. I think they're breeding. I miss you.

Buck

Sterling set the bag aside and rolled. On his side, he hugged the box and letter against his chest and stared at nothing, seeing everything. Too many nights to recall, Buck had held him while they told each other endless stories. They had known everything about each other, even down to the funny little dance Buck did while waiting for food to heat in the microwave. A sad smile tugged at Sterling's lips. For the life of him, he couldn't remember why anything at all had mattered more than their love. Sterling had pressed and pressed for some sort of big announcement about their relationship. When he looked back at things, he was pretty damn sure everyone actually knew. It wasn't like they were slick or even really tried to hide. Their love had been so big, it was like they were incapable of not touching each other. Then Sterling had left, and the ugliness inside his mind had beaten him. The emptiness always won. It was a dark hole, sucking every ounce of joy from him, turning his mind against him. Truth be told, the darkness was still beating him. Sterling didn't know how to stop it. He didn't know if he had any fight left.

Chapter Six

IT HAD BEEN WEEKS since Buck set eyes on Sterling. He was right down the road and across the street. Buck could walk to him in ten minutes and drive there in two. Sterling had to come to him. He had to be the one to choose. At least, Buck thought so. Fuck, he didn't know. He never knew shit. But Buck had sent a letter every single day. After sending a gift in the hospital, Buck started keeping Sterling up to date on the farm, telling him funny stories about the horses. Without meaning to, the notes had turned more personal. Buck couldn't help himself when it came to Sterling. He just wanted to hold him so goddamn badly. Hell, for all Buck knew, those letters had probably gone straight into the trash without Sterling reading a word. Still, Buck couldn't stop trying. If he hadn't stopped trying in the first damn place, everything could be different now. For all Buck knew, maybe Sterling would have married him. It was hard to say.

Dust fell from the ceiling.

Buck looked up, losing the threads of his thoughts. Someone moved around in the hayloft. Buck went on alert. It had been a long time since they had a trespasser on the property, but it wasn't unheard of. Buck quietly moved to the ladder. He didn't have his shotgun, but Buck was a big guy. There wasn't much that scared him. The guys were out in the field today. Quince was still with Jathan in the city. There shouldn't be anyone in the barn.

Buck poked his head into the loft just in time to see Sterling take off his shirt and wipe the sweat from his face. Damn. Buck's knees turned to jelly so fast, he almost fell off the ladder. Instead, he moved to step back down and let Sterling have his peace.

"Hey."

Sterling's greeting had Buck freezing in place. Buck's gaze returned to the beautiful body on display. "Hey."

"I thought the barn was empty."

Disappointment hit like a load of bricks. "It probably was when you got here. I just came in. I'd planned to run the horses today, but Quince still hasn't returned."

Sterling nodded. "How's it working out for you, being co-foreman?"

Buck climbed the rest of the way up the ladder and sat at the edge of the opening with his legs resting on the rungs below. "It's good. Honestly, I imagine the job will be a lot less stress on the both of us with backup. We can actually take time off without worrying. What have you been working on this morning?"

Sterling motioned toward the broom leaning against the wall. "Cleaning. When I was up here the other night, I noticed the bales were all over the place—like the guys have been grabbing stacks willy-nilly. Eventually, it would've gotten out of control with stacks being—" Sterling stopped and smiled. Buck's breath caught. He barely heard Sterling's next words. "Well, you know, since you do it all the time."

"One of the many things I've always loved about you is your willingness to jump in and help. It's not your farm or job, but you never seem to care about any of that."

Sterling shrugged, looking uncomfortable with the praise. "This is Tip's place. As soon as I turned eighteen, he built me a house to get me away from Mom. You know all that, though."

He did. Buck knew everything about him. "I can send someone else up here to do all this, if you want."

"It's all good. I need something to keep me busy and in shape."

What a gorgeous shape it was too. Buck was hot as hell, and it had nothing to do with the weather. Heat simply consumed him. He swallowed. Buck needed to move along and let Sterling be. "Then I guess I should let you get back to work."

Sterling never looked away from holding Buck's stare as he nodded. "You probably have a lot of shit to do."

Buck gave a sharp nod, as if the matter was settled. He had no idea why. It wasn't that things were uncomfortable. His unease was more due to not knowing where they stood any longer. Maybe they weren't even friends anymore. With an inner sigh, he moved to go down the ladder.

Sterling stopped him. "Hey."

Buck looked Sterling's way. He didn't want to hope.

Sterling shifted from foot to foot. "Would you like to have dinner with me tonight? I'll cook."

A smile exploded across Buck's face. The happiness that burst to life in him was next level. "You cook now?"

Sterling gave a half shrug. "Enough to survive on my own."

"I'd love to have dinner with you."

A slight smile touched Sterling's lips. "Six?"

"Works for me." Buck wouldn't have cared if he wanted to meet at two in the morning. He was there.

For a second, they held each other's stare. Buck had to force his feet to move. Everything inside him screamed to stay with Sterling. He had work to do if he hoped to make their date on time. Date. Fuck. Six couldn't get here fast enough.

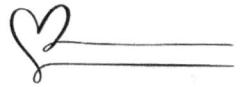

Sterling wasn't nervous exactly. He just wasn't sure if he was ready for this. Buck had sent him nonstop love letters since Sterling left the hospital. He had started a shoebox and the thing could barely close now from all the notes. One thing was clear now. Buck loved Sterling. Sterling had zero doubt on that point. The problem was Sterling. He was broken. At least he was self-aware,

When the knock came, Sterling was in the middle of running in circles, trying to remember everything he needed to do. Why had he offered to cook? He barely knew how to boil water. Sterling rushed to the door. When he pulled it open, everything else disappeared. Buck's dark brown hair was slightly windblown. A tight t-shirt stretched across his broad chest. Jeans cupped him just right. A hunger like no other hit like a semi. The overwhelming emotions were so much more than lust. Like in the barn earlier, love choked him. The love always eclipsed everything. Buck had been his obsession for so many years. No one else would do. Ever.

"Hi." Even Sterling heard how chipper he sounded, which was weird since he was stressed to the max.

"Hi." Buck moved his hand from behind his back. He held a casserole dish with a Tupperware lid. "Apple crisp."

Sterling's knees weakened. Buck's apple crisp was his absolute favorite dessert. No one made it like he did. Sterling didn't know what was different with his recipe, but he had never found one like it. He had tried.

Sterling took a step back. "Damn. You know that's my favorite. Maybe I should just turn off the oven and we can eat this. My cook—" The blaring of a smoke detector cut him off. Sterling froze for half a second before he remembered the mess going on in the kitchen. "Oh, no."

He darted for the kitchen. Heavy black smoke rose from the pot on the stove and even more smoke poured from inside. Sterling grabbed the pot and tossed it in the sink before ripping open the door. He grabbed the pan with no oven mitt without thinking. He immediately dropped the heavy pan on the oven's open door.

"Goddamn it!" The roared words barely left his lips before Buck had him steered toward the sink and held Sterling's hand under cold running water. The move immediately lessened his pain, but not his humiliation.

"It's okay. I've got you."

Sterling's gaze hit the floor. All he had wanted was a nice night. He couldn't do anything right.

Buck moved Sterling's hand from beneath the water to quickly inspect it before going right back to the steady stream.

"It's not that bad. Thankfully, it looks like you dropped the pan quickly enough to avoid anything serious. Don't move."

Buck rustled around behind him. The charred pan dropped into the other side of the sink. The alarm stopped. He heard the click and beeps of the oven being turned off. In no time, Buck was back. Sterling never looked away from the spot at the bottom of the sink where he didn't see much of anything at all. He had zoned out, trying to save himself from another mental breakdown.

Buck moved his hand from beneath the water again. This time, he turned off the faucet. He patted Sterling's hand dry. When he popped open the first-aid kit, a sliver of life returned. Buck knew where everything was in this house. At one time, Buck had practically lived here.

Buck spoke while he swiped burn cream over the wound. "I'm cool with just eating dessert."

Sterling couldn't even look at him.

"Or I could order us something," Buck added. "You'd be surprised how many people have started delivering out this way. With it just being me now, it's so much easier to get food that way than cook for only myself."

Sterling knew he should respond, but his throat was too tight to talk. He couldn't even look at Buck.

Buck didn't seem to need him. He kept going. "Speaking of which, I didn't make the apple crisp. I gave the recipe to AJ right after he moved out. The moment he started missing home, it was the first thing he asked for. I think he's perfected it a bit. He wants me to let him know if you prefer his. Actually, he was a bit giddy about it. I think he's convinced he's superior. Truthfully, he is, but I can't concede, and we need a tiebreaker."

At the first mention of AJ, Sterling's chin had lifted. The more Buck said, the more it sounded like AJ knew. "AJ knows you're here?"

Buck's gaze moved from Sterling's hand to hold his stare. His dark blue eyes always stared straight into Sterling's soul. "Yes. I told him everything. The funny thing is, as I said the words, I realized how idiotic I am. All this time, I never really hid us. As I told AJ I'm in love with you, it hit me. There was no way he didn't already know. There was no way everyone didn't know."

"Were you right?"

Buck nodded. "It's not like I called a meeting to make a huge announcement to everyone.

But it seemed like the moment anything happened to you, everyone came to me for updates and to ask if I was okay—like you're my other half and I feel your pain. They've all always known."

Sterling didn't know what to say. He didn't know how to feel. Part of him had always thought people likely knew, but he had always lived in fear of anyone saying a word. He had never been sure how Buck would react. Here they were. Buck acted like they had never been apart.

Sterling tried like hell to find the right words. A different truth fell from his lips. "My head still isn't very clear." He likely shouldn't have asked Buck to come here yet. Sterling couldn't help the craving that always came from his heart. "But I missed you. A lot."

Even though Sterling sounded dead, Buck obviously saw the sincerity in Sterling's eyes. "Come on. Let's sit down and order dinner. I just want to sit with you. That's one of the things I've missed the most, talking and spending every minute hearing your voice. Life has been pretty fucking empty without you."

"Okay." While logically Sterling knew he had only agreed to sit and talk, it felt a hell of a lot like he agreed to way more. Buck still felt like his other half. He was pretty sure they simply belonged to each other. It was a bit terrifying, realizing nothing either of them did could change that.

Chapter Seven

STERLING,

Last night was another night of staring at the bedroom ceiling while you lived inside my head. Do you remember the first time you stayed at my house for the weekend? AJ had spent the weekend with his friend. You brought dinner. I made love to you for as long as I possibly could. I saw our entire future together unfold. As soon as we sat at that dinner table together, I knew I had to have that for the rest of my life. I should've given you everything right then. That was the first time I failed you.

When you left, I knew you were done with me. You didn't deserve for me to treat you like a cheater. I knew I had finally broken us, and anger was all I had. It was easier to be mad at you than me, but in my heart, I'd always known better. I failed us. You'll never know how much I hate myself for being weak. You deserved the fucking world from me. I swear you'll get it. You'll get that life. If you ever take mercy on me and forgive me, I'll never let you down again. You'll have nothing but days of me touching you every chance I get while smothering you with words of love. Every night, you'll be in my arms while I tell you how much I'm addicted to every molecule of you.

I know I'm not the greatest with words. You probably don't even understand half of my ramblings, since that's exactly what I'm doing. I should describe the ways you brighten my life, but that's an endless list.

I wouldn't even know where to start. Once I start writing, all I can think about is the love that's choking me and the black hole in the center of my chest. I need you like I need oxygen. I have to believe—one of these days—you'll wake up next to me and that miracle will be forever. That hope keeps me alive. I'll never let it go.

I love you with everything I have,

Buck

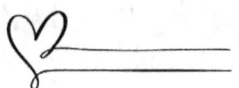

The love letters continued, confusing Sterling a little more every day. Despite the lines Buck wrote, it was like they were only friends when they were together. Sterling didn't know how to feel. He steered his horse through the woods, trying to clear his head. He heard the creek in the distance. Birds chirped. Sterling tried focusing on the sounds of nature rather than life. Everything felt heavy. The burden never lessened. There was so much he needed to handle and so little energy or desire to bother.

For reasons completely unknown to him, Coach Dale had stepped down from his position and confessed. His confession likely meant barely a slap on the wrist, but it also meant Sterling would never set eyes on him again. Sterling could go back to his career. Since the season had already started and Sterling hadn't returned, his agent and lawyers worked on the details. Meanwhile, Sterling decided if his mental health could withstand a season of nonstop gossip, intrusive interviews, and pitying looks. It would be so much easier to stay, hide, and try to reclaim some sort of life. Everything felt too hard.

Despite being back in therapy, Sterling had zero sense of normalcy. His therapist said his displaced feelings were likely caused by never feeling like any place was home. She was probably right. Sterling simply didn't know what it would take for him to feel settled.

The creek came into view. Sterling slipped from his horse and moved to the edge of the water. The sun glistened across the ripples, looking like a diamond when held up to the light.

Sterling found his usual rock and sat. His mind quieted and then drifted.

"I can see your ankles. Scandalous. We have to get married now if you want to protect your good name."

The look Buck gave him was priceless. It took everything Sterling possessed not to laugh. When he had quietly followed Buck down to the creek, he hadn't expected to find Buck with his shoes off, pant legs rolled up, and standing in the water.

"What are you doing out here?" Buck always sounded so growly with him. Sterling told himself Buck's annoyance was his way of telling himself he wasn't attracted to Sterling. But Sterling saw the looks Buck sneaked, and he knew lust when he saw it.

"I was looking for you."

"Why?" Ooh. The anger was getting bigger.

Sterling's smile never dimmed. "Maybe I hoped to catch you naked. A little birthday treat. You know how it is."

Buck's face screwed up in confusion. "Why in the hell would I be naked in the woods?"

Sterling shrugged. "Maybe you need to cool down after flirting with me all day."

Buck threw his hands up. He looked completely done with Sterling's bullshit.

Sterling was having the time of his life.

Buck made his way to the edge, grumbling under his breath. He angrily put his boots back on before focusing on Sterling. Rage flashed in his eyes. "Look, kid. You've got to stop this. I need this job and having you constantly hanging around will get me fired one of these days."

"I'm not a kid, and you won't get fired over me. Also, no one needs to know. You'd have a great time." Sterling felt the heat pouring from him. There was no way Buck couldn't see how badly Sterling wanted him.

Buck held his stare for a moment before turning away and taking a step toward the trail.

"Coward."

Buck froze. He visibly tensed before angry eyes turned his way. "What?"

Sterling shrugged, being as dismissive as possible. "I said you're a coward. You think I don't know we both want this? Your constant denials have nothing to do with your job and everything to do with your lack of courage."

The space between them disappeared. Nearly three hundred pounds of solid pissed-off cowboy went chest to chest with him. "One of these days, being a tease will get you hurt."

There was something very real flashing in Buck's eyes. For once, Sterling didn't recognize the emotion. He felt the rejection, though. That was as familiar to him as breathing.

Sterling took a step back. "I guess I misread the situation. You don't have to worry about me. As much as I like you, I get it. You don't feel the same. I thought you enjoyed our banter, and we were friends. I'm..." Sterling didn't know how to finish that. He was a burden. Sterling was invisible and pathetic. He was a pain in the ass no one wanted. All the above. He took another step back. "Sorry." Even he heard the pain he couldn't always hide.

Sterling turned to walk away.

Buck grabbed the back of Sterling's shirt and easily spun him back around. He was in Buck's sexy, muscular arms so fast, he didn't see it coming. Buck's mouth covered his, and Sterling stood still—like a frozen idiot. That barely lasted half a second. Then he melted. Buck's kiss was so much more than he expected. Sterling had expected Buck to kiss with unbridled lust and hunger. That *was not what this was. This kiss made the backs of his eyes burn. His throat swelled. He felt cherished. That had never happened to him. Buck cradled the back of Sterling's head, keeping Sterling from getting away without manhandling him.*

When Buck pulled away, he didn't release Sterling. "You drive me insane."

"I'm sor—"

"Stop talking, Sterling." Buck's mouth was back, blowing Sterling's mind with his kiss.

It hit Sterling. He wanted this for real. Sterling wasn't flirting or teasing. Not really. He was just so goddamn happy anytime Buck was around, he was like a kid on a sugar high. Except it wasn't sugar. It had always been something else. Something Sterling had never had before Buck. But God knew, Sterling had never felt the way he did about Buck with anyone else. All the way to his spirit, Sterling knew he never would.

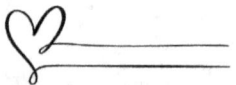

Sterling's horse, Lightning, trotted past Buck, returning to the barn saddled. Buck eyed the animal while his heart slowly crept into his throat. Buck stepped out and eyed the horizon. Lightning wasn't sweaty like he'd been on a long ride. Buck's gaze landed on a nearby trodden trail through the woods that led to a creek. The horses liked to go there to drink. Buck headed that way. His heart sped a little more with every step. Was Sterling hurt? Did he have another break? Fuck's sake. Buck couldn't handle this.

He saw Sterling sitting in his usual spot on a two-foot-high boulder. Sterling seemed to stare at nothing. It was obvious he was too lost in his head to hear Buck's arrival. Buck made as much noise as possible before squeezing his shoulders and massaging. "Your horse came back riderless. I got worried."

Sterling didn't respond right away. He cleared his throat. "Sorry. I guess I forgot to tether him."

Buck shuffled closer. Sterling's neck called to him. "You don't always have to apologize." His lips skimmed Sterling's nape.

Sterling took a shaky-sounding breath that went straight to Buck's cock. He knew that sound. "I was sitting here, thinking about the time you finally got angry enough to kiss me. You can't know how much I miss your lips on my skin."

Oh, damn. He was in trouble. Buck had been desperately trying to take things slowly. Not only had Sterling been through a lot, but Buck had fucked him with all the anger in his heart the last time they had sex. He hadn't known about anything Sterling had been through, and Sterling had at least pretended to like it. Sometimes, when it came to Sterling, he didn't know what was real or what was an act he hid his pain behind. Sterling was scarily good at play-acting genuine emotion.

Buck took a chance. He kissed Sterling's nape again. Without permission from his brain, Buck's hand slid from Sterling's shoulder to his throat. He gently held Sterling in place so Buck's mouth could explore exactly where he wanted. His lips moved from Sterling's nape to his earlobe. Fuck. He smelled amazing and tasted even better. Maybe this was a mistake. Possibly,

Sterling wasn't ready for this. Buck couldn't stop. He wouldn't until Sterling called it quits. Buck had ached for their love since the moment Sterling walked away. He hadn't been whole without him. As long as Sterling would let Buck touch him, he would.

"Damn, Buck." Sterling sounded breathless. "Don't stop. I want the man in those letters. Not the one who acts nervous around me—like you don't know you've always been everything to me."

Buck absolutely hated the way those words affected him. They reminded him of all the things they still had to work out. Sterling wasn't the only one who'd gotten hurt. Maybe Buck had deserved it, but that didn't change the way Sterling had broken his heart.

"I didn't know." The whispered confession tore at his throat.

Sterling stood and then reclaimed his seat, facing Buck. He looked aroused, and that nearly broke Buck. Sterling set his hands on Buck's hips and lured him into standing between Sterling's knees.

Buck instantly regretted having brought up the past. All he wanted was to be with Sterling. He shouldn't have risked their future on old hurts.

It was as if Sterling read his mind. "It's okay. You're right to be angry with me. Talk to me. I won't break."

His beautiful light green eyes cut right into Buck. Suddenly, he felt like letting everything go. But he knew Sterling wouldn't let him blow things off. They wouldn't be whole until they learned to communicate.

"I hurt you. You were right to leave me behind. You earned your career. I should've pushed you to go guilt free."

"But?"

He wanted to say there wasn't one, but they both knew that wasn't true. "The first time I saw a clip of you on someone else's arm, I was shattered. When you left, I guess I knew we were over. But there's always been a part of me that still thought we were forever. I thought we could overcome anything. Genuinely, I knew you'd be my husband. Then everything was gone. You crushed me."

"I know." Sterling didn't try to make excuses. "You deserved better from me. When I left, I knew I'd never love anyone else, and I should've clung to that."

"But you didn't want to be my secret." Buck knew where he had fucked up. "And you're right. You've never openly been the center of anyone's universe. To me, you've always been that, and you deserved everything I didn't give you. That's why I backed away and tried to let you find someone who gave you what you needed."

Sterling shook his head, but his gaze never wavered from holding Buck's stare. "There was never a chance anyone else could give me a single damn thing. Because you're what I need. Without you, every second has felt like dry drowning."

Buck hadn't known what Sterling could say to wipe away the way they had destroyed each other. Sterling had just said it. The seriousness Sterling showed said everything. He meant every word. Sterling was too much of a hiding-behind-jokes type of guy. He wasn't hiding now.

"I love you. You're all I want."

Buck nearly melted to the ground at Sterling's words. "I love you too. You're who I want to spend my life with."

Sterling cupped Buck's ass and urged him even closer. "I'm sorry I'm a mess. You have no idea how much I wish I was different. But I absolutely love you harder than anyone else ever could. I'm sorry about everything. If I had never gone to Miami, none of this would've happened. You wouldn't be looking at me right now and seeing all my mistakes. I wouldn't have—"

Buck kissed him, cutting off whatever painful words Sterling had been about to say. Nothing mattered except them at that moment. "We'll make new memories," Buck said between kisses. Buck had always been so in love with Sterling that he could hardly breathe. He never wanted to leave this spot and Sterling's arms.

Buck pulled away just enough to rest his forehead against Sterling's. He kept his eyes closed and simply absorbed the moment. They were touching. Buck's heart was overwhelmed.

Sterling squeezed his ass, reminding Buck Sterling still held it. "What now?"

A laugh burst from Buck. "I guess I get back to work before I end up fired."

A sexy, soft chuckle rumbled from Sterling. "That's not exactly what I meant."

"If you make me answer that question right now, I'll look psychotic."

Sterling's smile grew. "I am psychotic, so hit me with it."

Buck was already too deep to back down. "Your house or mine?"

"Absolutely any place, any time. Right here and right now works for me."

Buck heard the honesty in Sterling's response. Unfortunately, that wasn't what Buck had in mind... not that he would mind that either. "Okay. Yes, on your line of thinking, but that's not what I meant." Buck took a deep breath. "I meant, do you want to live at my place or yours?"

To Buck's absolute shock, Sterling didn't skip a beat. "My place is completely paid for, but I'm still willing to do whatever makes you the happiest."

That was a fair point, and Buck was over the moon. Sterling sounded as if he meant every word. "I guess it's your place, then. My house comes as part of my benefits package, but it's not mine. It belongs to the ranch. So it makes more sense to stay with you."

Sterling never batted an eyelash. He was obviously completely onboard. "Hey, no payment beyond insurance, since Tip pays the taxes, and maybe you'll get a raise in lieu of the house."

He was so serious and seemed to be thinking through every detail. Buck realized he smiled like an idiot. "It'll be easier to feel secure when you head back to Miami. I'll know you're coming home to me."

"That's another good point. When I sell the house in Miami, we'll have an awesome nest egg. Not that I don't already. My ten-goal rating has had me earning about eight mil a year for the past three years. We should be good."

Buck didn't understand. Sterling sounded like he didn't plan to go back to Miami. "What about your career? You worked your ass off for that spot."

Sterling's expression went from bright to a forced smile with heavy sadness attached. "You should probably get back to work.

I don't want to face anyone's wrath over hogging you all day. But do you want to come to our place tonight and start planning?"

Sterling already calling his houses theirs thoroughly distracted Buck for a moment. They had a little time to revisit Sterling's career. "I'll get there as quickly as I can."

"Good." Sterling's smile turned evil as he lured Buck closer. "One kiss before you go."

Buck nearly groaned. Sterling's one kiss was always enough to burn him to the ground. He would definitely spend the rest of the day fighting a hard-on. That didn't mean Buck didn't want that kiss. In fact, as Sterling's tongue curled around his, Buck quit caring about anything but the man in his arms. Their life would be amazing. No matter what came next.

Chapter Eight

Sterling stared at the water for longer than he cared to admit. It was as if he zoned out. Sometimes, it was like he was two people. When he was with Buck, Buck overshadowed everything, chasing away the voices in Sterling's head. The moment Sterling was alone again, he went back to overthinking every aspect of his life. He was trapped between both versions of himself.

Shaking his head, Sterling stood. He needed to get Lightning out of his saddle and brushed down before he went home. Sterling wanted to focus on tonight. There had been a lot of promise in Buck's eyes. Sterling craved the old, gentle Buck. The one who made love to him and swore they were forever. Sterling desperately needed Buck to take over his life and decisions. He no longer trusted his own mind. Sterling wasn't built to be in charge.

He reached his horse's stall just in time to catch Quince pulling the saddle from Lightning. "Hey. I was just heading in here to do that."

A bright smile flashed Sterling's way. Warmth settled inside Sterling's chest. Quince had always been like a father to him. Sterling loved him. Almost losing him had crushed him while he was already down much harder than he would ever admit to a single soul.

"Hey there, kid. I had an extra minute. How have you been?"

Sterling shrugged. He fought the urge to pour his heart out. His eyes burned at the thought. What if he'd had a real parent? Where would he be now?

Before Sterling could figure out how to answer, Buck raced into the stall. A laugh burst from Sterling as Buck's mouth covered his. His laughter quickly turned into fighting a moan. Buck pulled away, looking sexy as fuck. Their faces were still only about six inches apart. Love filled Sterling until he thought he would burst.

Buck took off his straw cowboy hat and placed it on Sterling's head. "Take this. Your face is burned."

Sterling groaned. "Great. More freckles."

"I love them." He kissed the tip of Sterling's nose and disappeared as quickly as he arrived.

When Sterling focused on Quince again, Quince was completely expressionless.

He finally blinked. "Um. What the hell was that? What did I miss?"

Sterling had forgotten Quince had been in the city with Jathan through all of Sterling's drama. No matter how hard Sterling fought, he couldn't stop smiling. "Oh. Sorry. I forgot you haven't been here." It hit him. Of all people not to know what was so obvious to everyone else, Quince was the last person Sterling expected to out of the loop.

Sterling shook his head as he eyed Quince. "Did you really not know?"

Quince still looked dumbfounded. "I haven't been around as much. For some reason, I thought you were dating German."

Sterling chuckled. "No. We're just friends. Buck and I have been together since I was nineteen. Off and on," he added reluctantly.

Unfortunately, Quince did not look happy to hear that. "Nineteen? He has a son nearly the same age as you."

It hit Sterling. This was exactly what Buck feared. Before recently, Quince had been Buck's boss. If Quince had realized they were together years earlier, he might have fired Buck immediately. Sterling saw the truth in Quince's eyes. He thought less of Buck now. That realization fired something dark inside Sterling to life.

"No." The word sounded harsh and cold even to Sterling's ears. That didn't stop him. "We fought too long and hard to be in a healthy place in our relationship. You won't ruin this by treating him differently now. He's the only thing keeping me sane." Plus, Quince was older than Jathan. If anyone should understand, it was him. Sterling didn't want to drag that point into the conversation, but he would if Quince said a single word against this relationship.

Quince eyed him. The tension slowly left Quince's body. Sterling watched Quince visibly relax. He dipped his chin, acknowledging Sterling's feelings. "It's all good. You two just caught me by surprise. I always expected you'd end up with some celebrity." Quince went back to work with Lightning. He spoke as he went. "A huge part of me expected you to disappear after moving to Miami. In a way, as much as it would've broken my heart, I kind of wished you'd never look back. I wanted you to find people who gave you everything you didn't have here. I hoped you'd find happiness."

Despite the conversation, a huge grin split Sterling's face. He brushed the horse, while seeing nothing but the images inside his head. "Being with Buck is the only genuine happiness I've ever known. Maybe I needed to see we weren't some case of me seeking love anywhere I could get it. I know better now. He's always been the only life I've wanted."

"Does that mean you're not returning to the team?"

Sterling shrugged. He hated this conversation, but at least Quince seemed willing to drop the whole Buck conversation. "My agent is looking into things for me. When he has all my options gathered, I'll have to make a decision. For now, I just don't know." Sterling genuinely didn't. No matter what he chose, there would be a downside. Either way, he ended up brokenhearted. Right now, Sterling wasn't strong enough to face that.

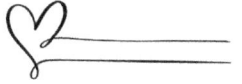

Buck leaned against the wall in the next stall and openly listened to every word. He had purposely kissed Sterling in front of Quince for a reason. Quince had always been the second reason—behind Buck's son—that Buck had kept Sterling a secret. He had never been sure how AJ would react, but he had known exactly how Quince would react. Quince was like a dad to Sterling. If Quince had learned the same news a few years ago, Buck would be out on his ass, and Sterling's relationship with Quince would have been altered forever. Sterling was much stronger now. A hell of a lot stronger than he had been back then. Sterling had handled the situation like a boss. Buck knew that was something Sterling needed right now. It was important for Sterling to get back to managing tough positions and knowing his own mind. Plus, Buck was just greedy and selfish. He had wanted to know if Sterling would hold his ground with Buck against the world. Buck couldn't be prouder of him.

When the conversation turned to other things, Buck got back to work. He had to check the fences and see if Quince had drawn up next week's schedule yet. If not, Buck didn't mind handling it. He understood Quince had been gone for a while. It might take some time for him to get back into the swing of things. Sterling lived in his mind as he worked. Love sat hard on his chest. Fuck. It felt like forever since he felt Sterling beneath him, looking at Buck like he knew Buck could move mountains. He was a little scared he would never have that again. Sterling had let Buck inside since his return, but that night should have never happened. Buck felt sick every time he remembered that encounter. Sterling had come home after being completely violated, only to have Buck treat him like a whore. Now Buck didn't know what to do. He didn't know what Sterling needed. He never, ever wanted Sterling to be scared or think of that piece of shit coach when they made love. Everything about Sterling had always made him feel completely out of his depth. Maybe he should wait for a while. That was probably for the best.

"Are you hiding out here?"

Buck nearly jumped out of his skin at Quince's quiet arrival. He did his best to hide his surprise. "Quince. Hey. No. I was checking the fences. It's that time of year."

Quince nodded. His nearly silver eyes cut through people. That feature especially wasn't comforting today. Despite his conversation with Sterling, Quince likely had some words for Buck. He was no longer in the position to fire him. Still, he had always thought of Quince as a friend. Buck didn't want to lose that.

"Did you know Sterling is considering not returning to the career he spent nearly his entire life striving toward?"

Buck nodded. "He's hinted at that."

"Is that because of you?"

Buck hadn't considered that. He assumed his departure from the team was fully on the head of that slimy bastard coach. "Not that I'm aware of." But it might be, and Buck needed to think about that. "I assume it's because of what happened to him."

Quince looked confused.

Oh no. He had opened a box he couldn't reseal.

"Why would a manic episode stop him from returning?"

Buck's shoulders fell. He already knew Quince wouldn't let this go. Buck sure as hell didn't want Quince approaching Sterling over the matter. Another thought occurred to him. How did Quince not know any of this? There had been a public confession and everything. The whole incident might not have as much coverage as Buck suspected. He had avoided the news like his sanity depended on it, because it did. Still, Quince's man was a huge basketball star. Sports news was likely a staple in their home.

Quince still stared at him, openly waiting for answers.

Buck cleared his throat. "Do you really not know? I thought the entire household had already passed around all of Sterling's business."

Quince shook his head. "I've been out of town and the guys don't talk to me like I'm one of them. They treat me like I'm their boss. All I heard from Tip—very reluctantly on his part—was Sterling had some sort of relapse. I could tell he didn't want to tell me that much, but I assumed that was because I was still healing."

Well. Shit. "I assumed it was all over the news."

"What was all over the news?" His tone said he wouldn't wait much longer before snapping.

Buck was trying his ass off here. The information Quince wanted was only an internet search away. Damn. It was best Quince heard the news from him. He cleared his throat again. "I wish you wouldn't make me say it. Sterling's coach drugged and raped him."

"What?" The deep growl to Quince's voice wasn't good for anyone. He didn't wait for Buck to answer what had likely been a rhetorical question. "I'll kill him. Jathan can afford to keep me out of prison."

Buck got it. He felt the same, but no one could help Sterling if they were all in prison. Plus, if they killed the guy, the case would get even more attention. Sterling needed peace.

"The guy confessed, which is why I'm shocked you haven't heard this. It was likely all over sports news channels."

"We rarely watch that. Jathan studies past games and whatnot, but when he spends time with me, he's spending time with me. What happened after he confessed? Is Sterling in counseling?" Quince paused for a second as the full ramifications seemed to settle in. "Is this why he came home and fell apart?"

"The guy is in prison, and yes."

Quince turned around for a second, as if he needed a moment to calm down without anyone looking at him. When he turned back, Quince looked devastated. Buck imagined he looked the same. The impact of the news never lessened.

"What can I do?"

Buck had to be straight with him. "You can pretend nothing has changed. Sterling doesn't want to go back because he knows how everyone will look at him. He knows this bullshit will be in his face every day, overshadowing every accomplishment he's made. He needs this place to be a soft, normal home."

Quince nodded. Buck could see in his eyes that doing nothing felt impossible. That was how Buck felt every night when he sat down to write the next love letter. The helplessness woke up alongside him like a second person living in his home. Every day, Buck felt useless as hell. He didn't know how to stop.

Quince motioned toward the fence. "Let's get this done so you can get back to him. I'm sure you're all he wants right now. The way he smiled after you plopped that hat on his head said everything. You're where his happiness lives. Right now is the time for you to focus on that. The schedule can lean heavier on me for a while. Sterling needs you."

Quince could never know how much that meant to Buck. Buck never knew if he did the right thing. He needed someone else to tell him what to do. If Quince thought Sterling needed more of Buck, then Buck was about to make the guy completely sick of him. It was time.

Chapter Nine

WHILE STANDING UNDER A hot shower, Buck stared at nothing, lost in his head. His entire body was lit like a firecracker, begging for Sterling's touch. No one could possibly understand what it was like for him to have Sterling's attention. He had been a single dad since AJ's mom had relinquished all rights the day he was born. Buck had taken one look at his newborn son and felt the weight of the world land on his shoulders, along with more love than he had ever felt in his life. It had been a struggle, staying afloat as a single dad. While, thanks to his parents, he had still found time to keep bed hopping, that hadn't lasted long. No one, male or female, had any real interest in a guy with a kid who was also nothing more than a farmhand. Then came Sterling.

The day Sterling had begun heavily flirting with Buck, he had been more than a little horrified. But Buck couldn't deny loving the attention and feeling desired again. He had never intended to touch Sterling. Little by little, every day, Sterling had broken him down. Each day Sterling flashed heated looks his way was another chink in his armor. Sterling was beautiful... and way too young for Buck. Except Sterling possessed an old soul since he had never truly been a child. Sterling had carried the weight of being the invisible and unwanted kid. He had such a playful personality, but when he looked at Buck, damn. That was a grown man staring at him. Everything about

Sterling was ten times more than anyone else. Sterling didn't care Buck was older or had a kid. He always treated Buck like he was just a man Sterling couldn't resist. That was fucking addictive.

Now Buck had to go to Sterling's and act like the proper gentleman. He needed to be there for Sterling as the man who loved him and supported him. Buck was scared he would fail. He missed the passion. Mindlessly, Buck's hand slid down his stomach until he gripped his cock. His eyes fell closed as pleasure ran through him. Behind closed lids, he saw the way Sterling always held his stare as he made his way down Buck's body. The heat in his expression as he swallowed Buck's erection was mind-melting. He was desperate to feel that hot mouth now, knowing they didn't have to hide. Knowing Sterling would be his husband. Nothing was just an out of reach fantasy anymore.

Buck stroked faster. He was already balanced on the edge of a knife. Buck had been too long without the slow way they made love. God, he craved the connection. His heart was famished. Buck's every breath came out as a pant. Sterling's perfect nude body filled his mind. Fuck, it was always so hot and tight on his dick. The way he kissed Buck's neck was enough to break Buck. The moment imaginary lips touched his neck in Buck's mind, a loud gasp tore from his lips. He stroked harder and faster, riding the ecstasy to the end. For a moment, Buck stood under the water, panting for breath with a completely blank head. Then the most invasive of all thoughts hit. What if he truly was the reason Sterling gave up all his dreams? If so, Buck had to live with that. He didn't know if he could.

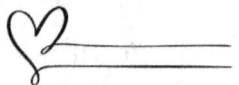

Sterling chewed the side of his thumbnail. Buck had texted and let him know he was on his way. His impatience was through the roof. Even on the best of days, it wasn't good to be alone with his thoughts. He needed a break from himself. Sterling had all the plans to lose himself. They all involved using Buck.

When the knock came, Sterling bolted to his feet and toward the door. He tried not to look too desperate as he pulled open the door.

Buck held a box. "I was thinking I should—"

Sterling grabbed two handfuls of Buck's shirt and jerked him inside. He captured Buck's mouth. The box hit the floor. Sterling went to work on Buck's jeans. He was already down to nothing but workout shorts. A lube bead did its job. Sterling was ready to go.

Suddenly, Buck tore his mouth away. He panted for breath. "Are you sure this is a good idea? I don't want you to—"

Sterling reclaimed Buck's mouth, refusing to hear whatever bullshit thing he had convinced himself was true. Buck hadn't touched him in weeks. Sterling couldn't take it. This was the one place he needed to feel normal. They were what kept him sane. Sterling had no trouble stripping Buck from his shirt. Unfortunately, that meant freeing his mouth for a moment.

"I just need to know this is really what you want."

Sterling went flush against Buck, letting him feel how much he wanted this. "I love you."

Buck's flushed face was sexy as hell. He didn't hesitate. "I love you too."

Sterling gave him a sharp nod. "Then trust me. This is what I wa—"

Buck had Sterling over his shoulder before Sterling could finish. Sterling hid a smile against Buck's back. Buck was so big and strong, taking up too much space. He always manhandled Sterling, but also made love like Sterling was precious to him. Buck had always been the exact thing Sterling needed for his battered soul. He carried the mental load, taking the hard decisions from Sterling. Buck was such a perfect place to feel safe. He was Sterling's home.

Buck gently placed Sterling on the bed. The way he looked at Sterling had Sterling's heart crawling to his throat. He shouldn't have left. Sterling never should have accepted that contract in Miami. If he had just stayed here with Buck, so many terrible things never would've happened. Unexpectedly, tears filled his eyes. His vision blurred.

Buck was there, holding him in an instant. He kissed Sterling's temple. "Shh. It's okay. I've got you. I knew it was too soon. I should've been stronger in my resolve and stuck with that."

It took Sterling a second to push words through his swollen throat. "No. That's not it. I'm sorry. Don't let me ruin things."

Buck pulled away enough to hold his stare. "You're not ruining anything. You're in my arms. That's all I've ever wanted from this life. You're my everything. This is all I need."

Sterling shook his head. "It just hit me how I ruined my life. If I hadn't left you."

"You would've missed out on a dream career while I still jerked you around. If you hadn't left, I might not be here now with my first box to move in. We might not be getting married. Hell, if you were smart, you'd be done with my bullshit way before now. You leaving and forcing me to see what I lost is what saved us. A lot of bad happened, but none of it is your fault."

Sterling clung to every word, desperate to hold on to his sanity. "I need you to make love to me."

"Baby, I—"

"I've already done the lube bead."

The neediness in Buck's eyes gave him away. He wanted this. "What kind of man would I be if I took advantage of you right now?"

Sterling wasn't having that bullshit. "You're not. I'm taking advantage of you. I need you

to hold me and make love to me. Please?"
He wasn't above begging. Sterling felt too
needy. The boy desperate for love inside
him was in charge tonight. He didn't know
what would happen to his mind if Buck said
no.

Buck's hand swept down Sterling's hip,
taking Sterling's shorts with him. The air
seemed to thicken. Buck stole the shorts,
leaving him nude. His heated gaze slid down
Sterling's body. Sterling nearly moaned at
the lust in Buck's stare. Buck moved away
long enough to strip away his clothes and
grab a condom.

"I jacked off before I came here so I
wouldn't fall on you with all the pent-up
need inside of me. Of course, it didn't work.
It's you. I swear there's something about you
I've never stood a chance against."

Sterling soaked up every word like a needy
sponge. Sometimes he thought there wasn't

enough love in the world to fill him. He was an empty vessel riddled with cracks. Sterling felt incapable of holding on to anything, but he would do whatever it took to keep Buck. "There's nothing special about me. But I absolutely love you more than anyone else ever could."

Sterling found himself covered in nearly three hundred pounds of cowboy. "Don't say that again." Buck looked intense as hell. "You are special. That's not just my opinion. You are loved by the people on this ranch, especially your brother and Quince. More than anything by me. You've got talent like I've never seen before. I'm willing to bet everything I own that teams all over the world are rubbing their hands together, waiting to see if you're up for grabs. Every day, I wake up knowing that you're so amazing, there's zero chance I'll get to keep you. You were always too important to spend your life with me."

He saw the moment Buck had talked himself straight into regretting Sterling.

Sterling gently pushed, urging Buck onto his back. He straddled Buck, forcing Buck to stay put. Buck looked like a runner. "No. Don't do that." Sterling kissed the corner of Buck's mouth, teasing him. "I'm supposed to be the fucked-up one. You're perfect." He kissed the other corner of Buck's mouth. "Only a fool would walk away from you. I won't be that idiot again." He swiped his tongue across Buck's bottom lip.

Buck opened for him.

Sterling took full advantage and control. One thing about Sterling: absolutely nothing could steal his desire for Buck. Buck was a sickness. Sterling craved staying just like this for eternity. Nothing meant more. While he had Buck distracted, Sterling quickly positioned himself and sank onto Buck's waiting cock. The ragged breath Buck took punched Sterling in the heart. His eyes started burning again. Their fingers linked as Sterling rocked himself against Buck, slowly taking what he wanted. The press of tears at the backs of his eyes grew stronger. This was what Miami had stolen from him.

Buck tore his mouth away. The horror in his expression made Sterling realize he was crying. His tears were on Buck's face. He looked horrified. "We should stop."

Frustration welled inside Sterling. He panicked. "No. Please? I need you. I need this."

Buck studied his face for a moment. He rolled and tucked Sterling beneath him. His gaze never wavered from holding Sterling's stare. "I have everything you'll ever need. It's a promise. You never have to beg."

"I know."

This time, they didn't look away from each other. Buck made sure Sterling stayed in the moment with him through every thrust.

"I love you."

Sterling gasped as the words seemed to mix with the way Buck moved inside him. There was nothing inside his head but an overwhelming love for this man and a slow building pressure that threatened to unhinge him.

"The way you look at me when I'm inside you, you stay stuck in my head all hours of the day."

Sterling's breathing quickened.

"Fuck. You're beautiful. I never get tired of staring at you. There's something inside you that glows brighter than everyone else. I want to touch it."

Goddamn. Buck knew Sterling had a bit of a praise kink. "I want you to touch it." Sterling didn't even know what they were talking about. But if Buck wanted to stroke any part of Sterling, he was in.

"When I'm inside you, I'm pretty sure our souls meet. No one makes me feel the way you do. It's like you were made for me. Just flawless."

Lord, he wouldn't make it.

"I want to watch you come unglued. That's the only time I'm certain you feel the same way I do."

Sterling fought to breathe. The winding inside him had him half insane. He thought he should argue with Buck's statement or something. Sterling kind of recognized he should reassure Buck, but his mind was gone. His tongue was busy whimpering.

"Let me have it."

It only took two more thrusts, and the world darkened at the edges of his vision. Cries and rambled words escaped him. Sterling fought for his life, writhing and digging his short fingernails into Buck's skin.

"Fuck, baby. Goddamn. You feel too good. I'm too addicted. Shit." Buck's final curse came out as a growl.

Sterling panted for air as he watched Buck come. Damn. He was sexy in the throes of passion. Sterling wished he could take a picture so he could take it out and savor the image anytime he wanted.

Buck's mouth clashed with his. Their kiss was so heated, it felt like he hadn't just blown. Buck always burned him to the ground. He knew Sterling's body.

"I need to hold you." Buck's confession came between kisses. Sterling couldn't give up Buck's mouth. He made Sterling's world disappear. That was the greatest relief he had ever known.

Buck didn't give him a choice. "I'll be right back." Buck climbed from the bed and headed for the bathroom. He came back sans condom and carrying a washcloth. The material was warm as Buck gently cleaned him. Sterling's heart swelled with love. There was no one like Buck. It felt like Sterling should say that. His throat wouldn't work. His emotions had him in a chokehold.

After tossing the washcloth in the hamper, Buck settled in with Sterling to hold him. Sterling savored every second. He loved the way Buck's heart beat and the way his breath brushed Sterling's head. Sterling adored the sensation of Buck's fingertips trailing back and forth against his skin. Goosebumps rose in their wake.

"Talk to me."

Sterling startled as Buck's words cut through the peace Sterling had found. A voice in his head screamed he didn't want to talk. His mouth had no such qualms. "I don't remember anything." It was too late. It seemed he was having this conversation. But the first words freed something inside him, and he couldn't stop. "Part of me wants to act like nothing happened. Then there's the rest of me that can't shake the fear and humiliation at realizing the truth. It seems like I should cower from touch or whatever, but it's you. None of this probably makes any sense to you. Even I don't know what I'm trying to say."

"You're making total sense." His voice was so soothing. Sterling closed his eyes and savored the timbre. "It's nowhere near the same, but when I was like eleven, I had an uncle corner me. Luckily, I got away before much happened beyond touching me inappropriately. Still, sometimes that memory sneaks up on me and horrifies me all over again. What you're going through is way worse, of course. But I get what you're saying. You don't remember the actual deed, but that doesn't stop the horror, but it didn't scar you in the bedroom."

Relief poured through Sterling. It felt good to be seen and understood. He nodded, squishing his face against Buck's chest. "Exactly. Part of me is permanently traumatized, but I just don't feel the way I think everyone expects me to feel. Then I feel guilty—like I should react a different way and maybe that means I'm even more damaged than I thought." Frustration grew inside Sterling again. He always hated the way he rambled too much while saying nothing and blurring everything.

"You're entitled to feel any which way you want about anything. You're in control. Fuck what anyone else expects. You're allowed to handle this however you need to." Buck gently lifted Sterling's chin to hold his stare. "I'll be with you for every step. We'll deal with whatever life throws our way—together."

Sterling nodded. He felt a lot better from simply getting to speak his piece. "Yeah. I don't really think we should wait long to get married." He couldn't give Buck time to change his mind.

Buck kissed him. The gesture was merely a sweet swipe of Buck's lips across Sterling's mouth. Still, Sterling's heart swelled with love and happiness.

"Whatever you want. It's yours."

A hum rose in Sterling's throat. "Mhmm. I like the sound of that. I think I can pull a third orgasm from you."

Buck laughed. "Oh no. I definitely should've skipped that shower fun."

An evil laugh escaped Sterling as he straddled Buck's body. He couldn't think of a single thing he would rather do than torture the love of his life. He had time.

Chapter Ten

BUCK COULDN'T STOP TRACING the shell of Sterling's ear. With Sterling's head in his lap, his feet kicked up, and a TV playing an old movie, Buck was in his version of heaven. They had only been living together for two weeks. Buck already knew he couldn't live any other way. The peace that had settled in his soul was unmatched. He finally had the exact life he wanted.

"I love you." Buck wondered if Sterling was sick of hearing those three words. They popped out hundreds of times a day without thinking. His heart was too full. It didn't have any other release. At least not one he could do a hundred times a day.

Sterling rolled onto his back. They had the front door open, letting the sunlight inside. The screen door kept out the bugs but let the cool air flow. Sterling might have money, but Buck had been poor his entire life. Electric bills got high.

The light streaming through the open door cast across Sterling's face. His pupils immediately constricted in the bright sun. His green eyes looked so big and pretty. Buck couldn't think about anything else. He brushed the back of his knuckles down Sterling's cheek. He couldn't even recall if they had been talking about something. Everything inside him was filled with obsession. He could stay like this forever and never notice the passage of time.

"I love you too."

Buck smiled. Oh yeah. That was what he'd said. "Can we stay like this and never move again?"

A luminous smile stretched Sterling's lips. "I'd love that, but I also adore moving around some with you."

Buck realized he smiled like an idiot. Damn. He was just thrilled with life. "You can do that too... whenever you want." Sexual promise hung in the air. Heat built between them as they held each other's stare.

"You're beautiful."

Buck's out-of-control smile might have made an immediate reappearance if he wasn't so invested in the growing lust. "Funny. I was just thinking the same thing about you."

"Good. We'll make beautiful babies." Sterling's goofy smile made Buck burst into laughter. Oh God, he loved this man so fucking hard. It was one of those things that would be just sickening to anyone within miles of their obnoxious fawning. Nothing else mattered. He was a full-on addict.

"I mean, I'm always game to try."

"We should—" A shadow disturbed the light on Sterling's face half a second before the doorbell rang, stopping whatever Sterling intended to say.

Both of their heads whipped toward the door. A tall guy wearing a business suit stood on the other side. "Sorry to bother you."

Sterling rolled to his feet and headed for the door. He didn't hesitate to let the guy inside. "Hey, Rocky. I didn't expect to see you today."

A loud groan ran through Buck's head. Rocky was Sterling's agent. He had only seen the guy from a distance and recognized the name, but they'd never met.

Rocky nodded at Buck before going right back to focusing on Sterling. "Yeah. Sorry for not calling. I was already here to talk to Tip. I took a chance you'd be here."

Sterling made a dismissive gesture. "It's fine. Come have a seat." He motioned Buck's way. "This is my fiancé, Buck. Buck, this is my agent, Rocky."

Rocky shook Buck's hand before sitting. His gaze stayed on Buck. "It's nice to finally meet you. Sterling has told me all about you."

Buck didn't know how to feel. A nervous laugh escaped him. "That can't be good."

Sterling huffed as he filled the spot next to Buck.

Rocky chuckled. "You've got nothing to worry about. I half expected you to be eight feet tall with the way Sterling always sings your praises."

Well, shit. He hadn't expected that. Thankfully, Rocky turned his attention to Sterling, so Buck didn't need to respond. "I've finished negotiating and lining up your options."

"Okay."

Buck linked fingers with Sterling to give him strength. Truthfully, he was the one who really needed it.

Rocky turned business-like. "While the team lost its right to demand non-disclosure thanks to the confession."

Buck was fucking grateful Rocky didn't say the bastard's name.

Sterling cut in. "Speaking of that. How did that happen? Why would he just confess like that? Not that I'm complaining, but he's probably done the same thing to other people countless times and gotten away with it. Why now?"

The evil smile that stretched Rocky's lips would have made Buck take a step back if he'd been standing. "I have some powerful clients. It was nothing to call in a favor."

Sterling looked as confused as Buck felt. "With who?"

Rocky shook his head. "My client list is extensive and colorful. It might include the Cattaneo family."

Sterling blinked. "Who?"

Despite being beyond blown away, Buck wouldn't leave Sterling in the dark. He bumped shoulders with Sterling and pretended to speak from the corner of his mouth. "The mafia, babe."

"Oh." Sterling merely sounded surprised. Otherwise, he seemed completely unbothered.

Rocky kept talking like nothing happened. "Anyhow, as I said, they've lost their right to demand non-disclosure from you. That hasn't stopped them from trying different avenues. As you know, you have a year left on your contract. If you want to play out the remainder of this year, you have to sign away your right to give interviews and whatnot on the matter. As much as I'd like to say that it isn't legal, in this case, it is. They are free to cut you loose and withhold the last eight million dollars you're owed to finish out your contract."

"For fuck's sake." Buck hadn't meant to speak out loud, but damn. "How dare them fuckers demand anything of Sterling?"

Rocky nodded as if he agreed. "On the other side of things, I was contacted by a publisher, asking for you to write a book. The numbers look pretty good."

"I don't know anything about writing a book." Sterling sounded defeated.

Rocky shrugged. "It's actually more like you're answering questions, and a ghost writer writes the actual book. If you don't want to return to Miami, this is an option."

Sterling looked his way. They held each other's stare. Buck swore he read Sterling's thoughts. He wanted to play the game he loved, but he loathed the idea of giving the team owners the satisfaction of silencing him. But Sterling also didn't want to talk about it and have his entire season be about his victimhood.

Buck tried comforting him. "I know."

Sterling's throat worked like he might cry. "I don't want to leave you again."

Okay. Maybe Buck hadn't known what Sterling was thinking. "You can't give up your dream for me. I'd always know it and hate myself for it."

Rocky cut in. "There's more. I have thoughts, if you're interested."

Sterling looked at Rocky like praying for a lifeline. "Okay."

"Your old local medium-goal team has reached out to me. They'd love for you to return. Obviously, they can't offer the kind of money as your current team does, but between the book and their salary, you'd come out better than finishing out your contract. You'd still get to play, and you wouldn't have to travel more than two hours one way in any direction. I think you'd have a better quality of life. Obviously, this means taking a step down, but—"

"I'll do it," Sterling said, cutting off Rocky.

Buck glanced over, trying like hell not to hope. He already felt sick and ready to break over Sterling possibly leaving again.

He found Sterling looking at him, as if waiting for Buck's attention. Like he needed Buck to understand why he had made the choice he had. "I don't love the idea of a book. But I understand it's important to speak up, so other people know they're not alone. And I can't leave you, baby. Not again. I might not survive it next time."

It seemed as if there should be some argument Buck should make. He couldn't. Things were way too real now. They weren't playing games or doing some sort of crazy tug-of-war any longer. They weren't a secret. This was very real. He wanted the future Sterling offered. "Me either." He knew his answer sealed the deal on Sterling walking away from a one-year multi-million-dollar contract. In his heart,

Buck knew this was for the best. Sterling really might not make it otherwise. That wasn't an option.

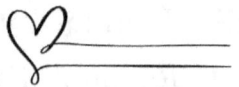

For the first time since Sterling came home, he felt at peace with his mind. His inability to decide his future had been tearing everything apart inside him. He honestly hadn't known what he could live with, but he knew what he couldn't live without. A weight had lifted off his chest. Sterling felt lighter and free. He never would have left his lower tier team in the first place if he hadn't convinced himself he would regret not moving up a rank for the rest of his life. That was a dream that didn't come true for many people. Sterling recognized the honor his hard work had achieved. But now, he also knew it didn't mean shit without Buck.

Sterling hadn't stopped holding Buck's stare since the moment Rocky left. He wanted to fall into those sexy eyes and drown. "There's another decision we need to make."

Buck didn't look away. "Okay. Hit me."

"I have a house to sell in Miami... unless you'd like to keep it and we could be snowbirds."

"I doubt that would go over well with Tip, considering Quince already has an all-over-the-place schedule."

"You know you don't have to work anymore, right? I might not be great at a lot of things, but I learned at my brother's feet how to grow money. Not to sound like that guy, but yeah. There's no reason to work."

Buck smiled. Laughter filled his voice. "Just like you, there's no way I can sit still across the street from the ranch and do nothing. It takes a massive amount of work to keep the place running. It may not be my land, but I've worked it long enough to care about its success."

Sterling shifted to his knees and straddled Buck's lap. "Well, I guess I'll just have to follow you around everywhere on my days off."

Buck ran his hands up Sterling's back. "I approve of this plan."

The way Buck bit his bottom lip as he towed Sterling even closer had butterflies stirring in Sterling's stomach. That was something he had never truly understood. It didn't matter how long they had been together or how familiar Buck's body was. Sterling never stopped getting that first-kiss flutter. He was so incredibly in love.

The heat built between them. Sterling lowered his head and brushed lips with Buck. "So fucking sexy."

"Nu-uh. That's you."

Buck's childish argument made Sterling smile. "I guess we'll just have to wrestle over it."

The wicked, soft laugh Buck released had chill bumps rising on Sterling's skin. He wanted to feel that on his cock. "What are the rules?"

Sterling tapped his chin as if pretending to think about it. "Hmm. I say we go down on each other and whoever blows first loses."

Buck's laughter-filled eyes were everything. "I accept your challenge."

Sterling slipped from Buck's lap and started to slither down Buck's body.

Buck stopped him before he made it to his knees. "None of that. I'm too fucking old to do this here." He stood and held Sterling's hand while he locked the front door and headed for the bedroom. Desire pulsed inside Sterling. His mouth filled with saliva at just the thought of sucking Buck's dick. His ass looked cute as hell in workout shorts. Buck had hilarious tan lines that Sterling adored. Everything about him screamed hard-working man, and damn. Sterling ate that shit up. He was half delirious with lust by the time they watched each other strip.

The instant Buck was free of his clothes, Sterling pushed him onto the bed and licked Buck's cock from root to tip.

Buck tugged his hair. "Nope. No cheating. We start at the same time, or the challenge isn't fair. Flip around here."

Sterling hid his smile as he did as instructed. He loved the way Buck took things so seriously. Sterling had always felt like he was the only man who existed in Buck's eyes. It was a feeling that was empowering as hell. He hoped like hell he made Buck feel the same. Buck's happiness was important to Sterling.

Sterling swallowed Buck's erection before he let insecurities sneak in and ruin the moment.

"Goddamn." The growled curse against his dick had Sterling positive he would lose this game. Not that it mattered. No matter what, they would both get off. That made them both winners.

Sterling gave everything he had, trying to match the pleasure Buck gave him. His toes curled. Sterling knew he was in trouble. There was no way he could hold out long with the way his cock sawed in and out of

Buck's mouth. The noises Buck made and the suction on his dick mixed with the way Buck fingered his ass. Sterling was tense as hell. Everything inside him focused on his release. It was right there. He was so close. Buck's mouth was so hot and wet. He was perfect. Buck hit Sterling's prostate and Sterling lost it. He cried out around his filled mouth. Sterling sucked hard—like he tried pulling more cum from his own cock.

Buck grunted and cum filled Sterling's mouth. It ran from the corner of his mouth. His brain had stopped functioning.

Sterling fought for air. The orgasm had taken him out. He panted, trying to hold together two thoughts and regain his brain power. "I want a rematch."

A bark of laughter cut through the air. "I love you so fucking much."

Sterling's cheeks hurt from smiling. Everything finally felt settled. He felt whole. The rest of Sterling's life looked bright as hell—filled with nonstop "I love yous" and gentle touches. Bring it on. He was ready.

Chapter Eleven

STERLING: *THE BED SMELLS like you. I don't want to get up.*

Buck: *Then don't. You're entitled to a day in bed.*

Sterling: *Then I won't be able to follow you around and bug you all day.*

Buck: *Mhmm. Bug me. I like it.*

Sterling: *Give me fifteen.*

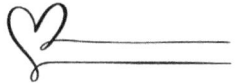

Buck: *AJ says he's gone to three stores, and no one has the champagne everyone likes.*

Sterling: *Tell him to get whatever is tolerable. As long as we're all together for the wedding reception, I'm not worried about what we drink.*

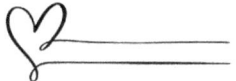

Sterling: *I can't wait to marry you.*

Buck: *I can't wait to marry you.*

Sterling: *Ha! We texted the same thing at the same time.*

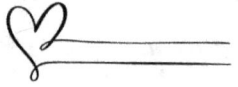

Buck: *How's practice going?*

Sterling: *Sorry it took me so long to text you back. I was out on the field. It's going great. A lot of my friends are still here.*

Buck: *That's great! I'm so proud of you.*

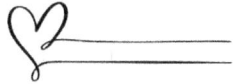

Sterling: *I love you.*

Buck: *I love you too.*

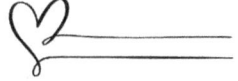

The way Sterling stood, completely at ease and smiling like happiness glowed from the inside, had Buck incapable of looking away. In uniform, covered in dust and sweat from the game, Buck was beyond ready to take him home. Buck knew he had done a lot wrong in his life and made countless mistakes. Sterling would never be on that list. The pride that filled his chest each time he looked at his sexy man, Buck wanted to point and scream, "That's my man!"

The moment came that was always inevitable these days. Buck held his breath the second he heard the question hit the air.

"Do you think your old team is missing you now since their season tanked?"

Sterling kept the perfect, nonchalant expression. "I have no idea."

"Do you think their season was impacted at all by the release of your book?"

Sterling shrugged. "I seriously doubt it, but if so, I don't care. My book empowered several other victims to step forward. I'll never regret standing up for what's right and not allowing them to force me into silence. I can't even imagine what it takes to be so horrible, you'd bully a victim."

The blond reporter nodded along. She continued talking, but Buck couldn't hear anymore. He was too focused on Sterling's expression, praying this didn't trigger a rebound. While Sterling was a thousand times better than he had ever been, mental health didn't always care how good things were going. Battles against the mind were some of the toughest.

Sterling's gaze flickered his way. He said something to the interviewer. After a few exchanged nods, Sterling headed his way. Buck didn't hesitate. He opened his arms for Sterling.

Sterling walked into his embrace. He stole a quick kiss. "Hey."

Buck couldn't stop smiling. "Hey. You did great today. Congratulations! You'll probably end up with more offers to move up in the league than you can handle after this." Sterling had helped his team win every game of the season, but two they had before he was added to the roster. A pro taking a step back into a lower league, at the height of his career, was obviously more than his opponents could handle.

Sterling kissed him again until he pulled away, breathless. Love stared at Buck. "It doesn't matter. I'm not going anywhere." His gaze raked Buck's body. "Why would I leave all this behind? Plus, there's no way I can sleep without my husband keeping me warm."

A loud cackle cut through the air, making them jump. They turned to see Tip, AJ, and Tip's husband Artem headed their way. Artem pushed his grandmother Baba's wheelchair. It seemed she had been the one to shock them out of the moment.

She clapped. A huge grin split her face. She was a naughty old gal who spent half her time living at the ranch with Tip and Artem. Buck loved her. Everyone did.

"A game and an after show. Don't stop on my account."

"Stop on mine," AJ said with a laugh. "I'm too young to witness this."

Baba let out another witch-like cackle before smacking AJ's arm. "Don't be a prude, boy."

AJ's smile screamed he wasn't bothered. He had spent a lot of time with Baba before moving out on his own. She was as good as his grandmother too. "It's not prudishness to not want to watch your dad making out."

Baba shrugged. "Fair."

Buck shook his head.

Sterling moved to hug Baba.

Tip patted his back. "Good job out there."

Sterling deserved to be exactly where he was: the center of attention. He made a dismissive gesture. "I had fun, but I'm also glad it's over." He tossed a glance Buck's way before continuing. "I'm ready to relax for a while."

A shiver of delight ran down Buck's spine. The look of promise in Sterling's eyes screamed there would be little relaxing.

"This was fun. I had a good view of all the sweaty men."

Artem shook his head but looked resigned. His grandmother was always a mess.

Sterling chuckled. "There's always next year."

"Speak it into existence, boy. I'm old."

Buck couldn't stop fighting back the laughter.

Baba made a dismissive gesture. "Today is about you. Speaking of which, I read your book. Then I had Tip drag out my cauldron." She patted Tip's arm. "We make the best spells together." She focused on Sterling, turning serious. "That man will not have a good time in prison. No, he absolutely won't."

Sterling looked uncomfortable for the first time. A nervous laugh escaped him. "Thank you." He sounded as if he wasn't sure if that was the right response.

Baba gave him a sharp nod.

Buck stepped in before Sterling withdrew. "I thought we were going to dinner."

Baba nodded. "I'm starved. That German fellow said there's some roadside bar and grill place around here. This old lady needs a drink."

Artem backed up Baba's chair. "Then let's get started. If a drink is what my lady wants, then that's what she gets."

The happiness in Baba's laughter made Buck smile. She might be a scandalous one, but she was also well loved. He hoped for the same in his golden years.

AJ squeezed Buck's shoulder before shaking Sterling's hand. "You did great. See you two at the restaurant."

Buck did all the smiling, nodding, and pleasantries. It was fantastic to see his son being so okay with Buck's marriage. But it was a huge relief when he finally had Sterling alone in the truck, especially since Sterling was across the cab and on him in an instant. Their tongues stroked. Heavy breathing filled the air. Sterling kept him so hot, he thought he would explode.

"How late do you think we can be before they get suspicious?"

Buck swallowed and adjusted his erection. "Not long enough."

"Damn."

Buck nodded. "Same."

"Let's hurry, then."

Buck put on his seat belt while Sterling did the same. "Agreed. One drink. Quick bite, and then home."

As if reality hit them simultaneously, they froze and held each other's stare. Time seemed to halt. They were really okay. Happy. Deliriously happy. Too many times over the years, Buck hadn't seen a path for this life. Somehow, life's challenges hadn't broken them. Their love was stronger than the ugly parts of living. This was meant to be. They were soulmates and best friends. Unbreakable.

"I love you."

Sterling's words cut through the spell that kept him frozen.

"I love you too."

Sterling swallowed. "I was so damn scared we'd never have this life."

Buck nodded. "Me too."

They linked fingers. Another moment of savoring their marriage passed before they made the drive to meet their family. Their family. The miracle of them never ceased to amaze him. Thank God. The alternative was unthinkable, but their love was indestructible. That was a proven fact. They were forever.

German's book will be part of my series, Steel Security. These showcase some of the toughest bodyguards in the country as they fall hard for men they never see coming. The first book in the series is *Finding Shelter*.

About the Author

CHARITY PARKERSON IS AN award-winning and multi-published author with several companies. Born with no filter from her brain to her mouth, she decided to take this odd quirk and insert it in her characters. One of her greatest loves is writing morally gray characters. You'll find them scattered throughout her hundreds of titles.

*Nine-time Readers' Favorite Award Winner

*2015 Passionate Plume Award Finalist

*2013 Reviewers' Choice Award Winner

*2012 ARRA Finalist for Favorite Paranormal Romance

*Five-time winner of The Mistress of the Darkpath

Connect with her online:

*Sign up for her newsletter: https://bit.ly/charityparkersonnewsletter

*Join her readers' group on Facebook: http://bit.ly/CharitysTribe

* W e b s i t e : https://www.charityparkerson.com

*A list of her social media accounts and giveaways all in one place: http://hy.page/charityparkerson